Narralogues

SUNY series, The Margins of Literature

Mihai I. Spariosu, editor

NARRALOGUES

truth in fiction

Ronald
Sukenick

STATE UNIVERSITY OF NEW YORK PRESS

Some of the pieces in this book were originally published in *Iowa Review*, *Black Ice Magazine*, *Boulevard*, *Denver Quarterly*, *New Letters*, and *Talus*. "What's Watts," "Divide," "Death on the Supply Side," and "Name of the Dog" appeared in previous Sukenick collections.

Published by
State University of New York Press, Albany

© 2000 State University of New York

For information, address State University of New York Press, State University Plaza, Albany, NY 12246

Production, Laurie Searl
Marketing, Dana Yanulavich

Library of Congress Cataloging-in-Publication Data

Sukenick, Ronald.
    Narralogues : truth in fiction / Ronald Sukenick.
        p.   cm. — (SUNY series, the margins of literature)
    ISBN 0-7914-4399-X (hc. : alk. paper). — ISBN 0-7914-4400-7 (pbk.
    : alk. paper)
        1. Experimental fiction, American. 2. Narration (Rhetoric)
    I. Title. II. Series.
    PS3569.U33N37 2000
    813.009—dc21   99-39774
                                                                         CIP

10 9 8 7 6 5 4 3 2 1

for
Waldos and Waldosas
everywhere

Contents

Introduction   1

Gorgeous   9

Chat   15

A la Bastille   27

Art Brute   35

Dick and Eddie   49

Narralogue on Everything   61

What's Watts   101

Divide   105

Death on the Supply Side   113

Name of the Dog   121

Introduction

"It's Only
Make-Believe"

A narralogue is essentially narrative plus argument. Narralogue differs from dialogue—a term whose critical utility has been re-established by the work of Bakhtin—in that it gives full play to the element of action that is essential to narrative, and action takes time, which is the enemy of abstraction, formalism, and dialectic. The action in question, of course, is the action of mind meditating event, generated by what is normally called imagination, but which might be more fundamentally called the quarrel of consciousness with time. The unfolding of argument through time allows something like Bakhtin's concept of "dialogized heteroglossia" to come into play, making absolutes and definitive form seem naive and simplistic.

Significance is established in narrative—as opposed to plot—by accretion as well as by endlessly deferred meaning rather than by conclusion. Part of my argument in the *Narralogues* is that narrative is a mode of understanding that uniquely is quick enough, mutable enough, and flexible enough to catch the stream of experience, including our experience of the arts. I might even claim that my narralogues model a kind of criticism. But this is not the point, which is to bring what we call fiction into consideration as a mode of thought under the umbrella of rhetoric. Rhetoric is meant here not as a system of classification, heavily terminological, as in the work of Harold Bloom, however dynamic, and even less as the study of oratory or ornament. Rather, it is meant as a kind of ongoing persuasive discourse that, in itself, resembles narrative—agonistic, sophistic, sophisticated, fluid, unpredictable, rhizomatic, affective, inconsistent and even contradictory, improvisational, and provisional in its argument toward contingent resolution that can only be temporary. In

1

fact, it is a discourse not unlike the poetry of John Ashbery, which I regard as highly rhetorical. Rhetoric comprises a discourse, I would argue, that most resembles the way we normally process experience and is therefore most suitable to catch on to experience, participate in it, and help sort it out.

In short, my argument is that fiction is a matter of argument rather than of dramatic representation. True, drama employs argument and fiction employs representation, but I'm talking about defining qualities. This, with certain points of difference, is a tack taken recently by Richard Walsh in *Novel Arguments*, where however, it is applied only to innovative fiction. My point is that all fiction can be profitably regarded as argument. When you define fiction by representation you end up confining it to realism at some level and arguing that fiction, as a form of make-believe, is a way of lying to get at the truth, which if not palpably stupid is certainly roundabout and restrictive. My approach frees fiction from the obligations of mimesis, popularly, and most often critically, assumed to be its defining quality. However, mimesis is more consonant with the theater, and while fiction makes use of mimetic representation, it is not confined to it. Fielding, who came out of the theater and promoted a representational approach both in theory and practice, nevertheless wrote didactic novels which at the core are arguments for a certain point of view. Sterne, who came from the pulpit, in my perspective was closer to the essential of fiction with a self-conscious use of language and a feeling for it as persuasion, an ironic view of representation and an explicit use of rhetoric, none of which prevented him from constructing effective dramatic scenes. Both Plato and Aristotle made a distinction between the wholly mimetic form of drama and the partly or nonmimetic form of other genres. I view mimesis as an element in the rhetoric of fiction, on a level with the element of scope, which reminds us of fiction's heritage from the epic with its recited, rather than theatrical, base. The rhetoric of fiction is a rubric that covers the studies of Wayne Booth as well as the recent field of narratology, which might be considered the application of a new rhetoric to the essentials of narrative. However, it is the mutability of consciousness through time rather than representation that is the essential element in fiction, and the rhetorician who seems to catch this best is Kenneth Burke, with his concept of "swerve" and his sense of literature as a form of persuasion.

But the foregoing perspective is not one I arrived at on the basis of theory, about which I know nothing—rather, it came to me in consequence of my experience as a practicing fiction writer. It all began when, to my surprise, an editor accepted one of my stories but insisted on listing it in the table of contents not as fiction but as essay. This genre confusion recurred, not only with editors but in other ways. After a reading at a university a professor got up and said, "I like your piece but what's the difference between this and personal essay?" Evidently, I had crossed some line beyond which, in our tradition, narrative ceased to be recognizable as fiction. Reflection is not part of the standard repertoire of recent American fiction, despite lip service to the spirit of Hawthorne, Melville, and Henry James. The reasons for this are multiple, but the driving force behind the taboo against thought is money—reflection gets in the way of narrative as mass market entertainment. The blockbuster requires a quasi-hypnotic level of make-believe. But this is not the point. The point is that even narrative as reflection of "reality" is still reflection in both senses. It is not merely that *The Sun Also Rises* advances an agenda as surely as does *Pilgrim's Progress,* but that in doing so it raises issues, examines situations, meditates solutions, reflects on outcomes—that is to say, the story line is itself a form of reasoning. The question is only whether a story reflects thoughtfully, or robotically reflects the status quo with no illuminating angle of vision of its own.

Once the "mirror of reality" argument for fiction crumbles, possibilities long submerged in our tradition open up, and in fact a new rationale for fiction becomes necessary. There is no longer any excuse for confining fiction to plot-character-description in noncommittal plain style zip zip zip between margins to the bottom of the gutenbergian printed page. For one thing, if fiction is a way of thinking—as reflection, experimental enactment, rhetoric—its form becomes as potentially various as the forms that thought takes. And if thought is fundamentally a way of deriving conviction from experience, then persuasion is clearly a basic form. We begin to inquire as to the virtue and necessity of fiction to start with, and here again we discover untapped potential that turns on dissolving the misleading opposition of "fiction" and "truth." Fiction is no longer an imitation of the supposedly real, but has a reality in itself whose purpose is to reflect on experience to arrive at truth, however contingent. That fiction is an instrument for arguing truth is an apparent paradox I decided to exploit. Thus, the narralogues.

I had long noticed when a fictive narrative appears to be pursuing a course of persuasion with regard to truth it loses its make-believe status and tends to be shunted into some bastard category such as "faction," "creative nonfiction," or personal essay. But there is a continuity among kinds of narrative which is more essential than the prescription of representation in fiction. And there are many narrative options among the possibilities of imaginative writing that may be plausibly categorized as fiction within a less constricted definition. This becomes evident when one considers narrative writers in the Western tradition who write more out of the rhetorical line going back to Aristotle's *Rhetoric* than the dramatic line of narrative evolution descending from Aristotle's *Poetics*, such "novelists" as Rabelais, Sade, Sterne, Diderot, Rousseau, or in the modern period, Proust, Joyce, Stein, Shklovskii (in *Sentimental Journey*,) Bataille, Beckett, and Henry Miller. These writers combine the two lines of evolution in a variety of ways, and their work may yield fresh insights when regarded from a rhetorical point of view. While it cannot be denied that the dramatic-representational line has been dominant, especially in Anglo-American fiction, the possibility must be considered that it is beginning to approach the limit of its utility in our culture. Postmodernism in fiction may be considered, in part, a rebellion against the constraints of mimesis in favor of a return to the rhetorical tradition. Certainly the revolution of the computer screen against the printed page, with the screen's tendency to force a view of writing as a plastic as well as a transparent representational medium, promotes a view of language itself as subject to rhetorical manipulation. Such developments as Postmodernism, chaos theory, and fractal geometry come out of a changed consciousness of the way things happen. Richard A. Lanham, in *The Electronic Word*, argues that rhetoric, resembling a nonlinear system as a "constantly changing emergence rather than a fixed system" that "considers human behavior as complex beyond prediction and yet subject to certain rules, and one which for that reason emphasizes the improvisational ability," offers the best chance of capturing that new sense of reality. In the fluxy world of Postmodernism, fiction needs to be less representational and more rhetorical.

When I first started writing fiction, I had no sense that my writing career would span a breakthrough to a new rhetoric of narrative.

I expected my writing to develop in much the same way that, say, Philip Roth's was to do, basically extending the so-called realist strain in fiction with a new content pertinent to my generation. I can't explain why my writing took a different course, except to say that things did not seem to happen to me the way they happened in the books I read. When I started writing out of my experience rather than my literary background I was surprised and, in a certain way, pleased at the vitriolic response from some quarters. I had not expected the explosive consequences of fiddling with the authority of the gutenbergian page and the Aristotelean plot. Of course I realized they supported a particular way of life, but it wasn't mine. As Pierre Bourdieu reminds us, "on doit se garder d'oublier que les rapports de communication par excellence que sont les échanges linguistiques sont aussi des rapports de pouvoir symbolique où s'actualisent les rapports de force entre les locuteurs ou leurs groupes." My commitment to experience rather than literature provoked charges of "solipsism" from people who thought that the going literary forms represented reality when they only represented the status quo. The most vexing criticism came from left wingers who thought my work didn't come to grips with political reality, while my sense was that our forms of discourse—which explicitly concerned me even then—embodied our most profound, if veiled, political investments. I gradually came to see imaginative writing not as the fabrication of make-believe versions of a debatable reality, but rather as a way of salvaging experience from overbearing and intrusive discourses whose aim was to manipulate one's sense of the world in somebody else's interest. Rhetoric can be the blunt instrument of power.

In particular, I began to see fiction as a potentially serious enterprise rather than a form of entertainment. I realized that the pleasure and excitement that I derived from some novels was attributable to the way they helped me understand my experience and live my life. In other words, for me fiction had always been a way to knowledge rather than a way to goof off. I believe the same is true for many readers. A rhetorical approach to fiction once again allows the intellectual space to accommodate those readers. While not conceding the realm of pleasure, narrative as rhetoric, in its consideration of relation to an audience, is interactive, the Wordsworthian "man talking to men," as it were, and more frankly democratic in its literary aspect than narrative as entertainment, which encourages a hidden intellectual passivity.

Among other advantages, the rhetorical tradition offers the possibility of reconnecting fiction with other serious discourses of knowledge in the culture, rather than keeping it segregated as a sort of make-believe partitioned by half-baked notions of the willing suspension of disbelief. Within the rhetorical tradition it is easy to see the continuity of fiction and law, which share many traits by way of constructing persuasive narratives. The mutual recognition growing between the two fields can be seen in the "law and literature" movement. From another point of view, by considering fiction within the rhetorical tradition, one can apply to it truth evaluations in the same way that one considers the truth value in any other serious discipline. We can judge the truth of fiction in the same way we can consider the persuasiveness of any argument. I would argue that even the esthetics of style must be judged on the basis of truth value. So in the rhetorical tradition fiction becomes a mode of thought—just like any other serious discourse. Narrative thought is, moreover, a powerful form of discourse if only because we all make use of it as we create our own life stories from our experience. It can, as we all do according to temperament, exploit all the modes of traditional fiction—comic, satiric, dramatic, tragic, pathetic, erotic—to couch argument in the foundation of experience. As we interact with experiential situations through narrative we project models, trial balloons, so to speak, that participate in those situations and feed back information about them. But, also, situation tempers abstraction with history. For these reasons, as in the Platonic *Dialogues*, which are of course the remote progenitor of the *Narralogues*, I couch each narralogue in an experiential situation. Narrative cuts against the grain of the kind of abstraction I deal with here and grounds it in the grit and knit of the experience it must ultimately be based on.

As I sit here at my computer keyboard, I am more aware than I want to be of my other professional activities, most of which have to do with the same principle that I'm concerned with here: the promotion of narrative as thought and articulation as against narrative as mind-numbing make-believe. I interrupt this composition to make three phone calls in my identity as a small press publisher concerning ways of bucking the commercial conglomerate publishing industry to get into print books of quality fiction that probably won't make any money. The validation of serious fiction as against the flood of junk from the conglomerate entertainment giants is not an "academic" matter to me. I am not engaged in a theoretical struggle with imaginary windmills but in an uneven battle with real monsters. This kind of battle, fought by too few against odds that are too great, has real consequences in determining whether a free intellectual discourse will be able to continue in this country. Part of the fight is to restore for narrative art an intellectual rationale that has been overtaken by the age and become unconvincing. The perspective explored here offers the possibility of a narrative that does not need the insubstantial justification of mimetic illusionism. The common notion of fiction as a form of pure fabrication rather than a discipline of knowledge has been undermined by developments in theory, and increasingly so in the practice of fiction, especially in the United States, since the advent of *Naked Lunch* forty years ago. Nevertheless, fiction as make-believe is massively promoted by the publishing conglomerates and the electronic media, and leaves narrative vulnerable to total usurpation by the entertainment industry. Contemporary culture is swamped by hegemonic narratives in the guise of "entertainment." If we are to revive a critical and ethical counter force, we must move away from "spectacle" (Debord) and "simulation" (Baudrillard), and in the direction of the arts—and especially "fiction"—conceived as argument about experience rather than facsimile of it.

Of course I'm being totally disingenuous about all this. In a way. Obviously I'm promoting a kind of fiction as well as a manner of regarding fiction in general. But there's a certain sluggishness in the transition from intellect to taste and you can't argue anybody into liking anything. Wasn't Bergson said to prefer realist fiction to Proust's work though the latter had been influenced by his own? I imagine you as sympathetic reader reading this essay, possibly assenting to it or maybe partly so, and then reverting to Jane Austen, Hemingway, or even Ray Carver on a dare. Or maybe detective stories are what you read for real pleasure, nothing wrong with that. Nobody can carp about what happens to seduce you. Can they? The rhetoric of argument is a sledge hammer compared to the finesse of the rhetoric of seduction. But seduction is part of the argument, is it not? And people enjoy being seduced when the right calculus of desire comes along. Personally, I prefer seduction to deduction and I'm sure you do too. And seduction requires spontaneity, improvisation on the instant feedback you get from the object of desire. That's why, when you embark on an erotic adventure—and all art, as opposed to theory, is an erotic adventure—it doesn't pay to have too many fixed ideas in your head. So do your best to forget everything I've said. Instead I invite you to become a participant in what follows. Feel free to disagree, to make your own arguments, to curse or bless me as you wish. It's all part of the ball game, and some people come to the ball game just to yell at the umpire. Anything to make you happy, dear reader—as they used to say. Because you are the object of my desire. I love you. Yes, reader dear, it's true, I've got the hots for you. I know it's scandalous, but what can I say? I too am astonished at this turn of events. But what the hell—it's only make-believe.

Gorgeous

They were walking through the valley of Gehenna, toward the Jaffa Gate of the Old City in Jerusalem when Esau, who was a native, started making fun of the exiles.

"They're ashamed of themselves," he said. "There's this old joke about a family trying to assimilate into America, plenty of money, but manners are still a problem. So they're having this big dinner with their upper crust WASP friends and the husband tells the wife to cool it and lay off the yiddishisms. In the middle of the dinner the maid walks in with the ham on a tray, trips, and drops it on the floor, whereupon the wife exclaims, 'Oi vay!—whatever that means.'"

"Very funny," said Jacob. "But it's easy to make fun of people trying to fit in. And why shouldn't they fit in? Such people go to schools that are in the English and German tradition going all the way back to the Greeks. In college they join Greek fraternities. They study Plato, not Maimonides or the Kabbala. What do you expect? They aren't trying to be assimilated, they are assimilated."

"So much the worse," said Esau. "Because that's just a tradition of smoke and mirrors. Tricks. But the day is past when you can pull the wool over our eyes, Jacob. Like that fraud you conned our father with. Hairy forearms shit. Where did you pick that one up, Plato's Cave?"

"What's wrong with Plato's Cave?"

"Plato's Cave must have been a bar where he went to get drunk on retsina till his mind began playing tricks on him. Tricks that people with your Judeowasp attitude seem to take seriously, when he must have meant them as something like speculative jokes. Or maybe he actually believed what he was seeing, even though he knew it wasn't the real thing. But I don't think so. After all, he knew he was dealing with imitations. The only thing is, he claimed they were imitations of the real thing. That everything was an imitation of those supernatural Platonic Ideas. That's where the retsina comes in. Because he more or less admitted the real thing was fake. Just an idea."

"You're an anti-intellectual?" said Jacob. "Besides being a shit kick nomad?"

"You're referring to the fact that I started out as a shepherd while you were a farmer? So that you ended up owning the land while I was rootless? Forced to move from place to place? Well let me tell you a thing or two. First of all we're all wanderers now. That's the nature of hypercapitalism, postmodernism, the information age, the electrosphere, whatever you want to call it. We're dynamic entities in a mobile medium. Only a dumb farmer could swallow that Platonic business about static and permanent abstractions of which everything else is pale imitation. And you know why? Because farmers have to stay in one place. Down on the farm. Only immobilized people need immobile ideas. But what are you going to do when agribusiness moves in? And besides, how ya gonna keep em down on the farm after they've seen Paree? If only on TV."

"You know what you are?" asked Jacob

"No. What am I?" replied Esau.

"You're a subversive. You're trying to undercut two thousand years of Western Civilization, the tradition of the Humanities, the tradition that gives dignity and importance to the Human Race."

"The Greco-Christian tradition that ended with the Holocaust, if not earlier, with World War I, for example, or you could go further back because this was always a tradition mainly used for lip service while the wise guys went on with the real business at hand, namely, exploitation, oppression, rape, and murder. A tradition whose reigning coin was hypocrisy."

"The tradition that brought us our great books, music and art, and our whole conception of human rights, in fact, of humanity."

"Except, for human rights you need humans, and we are clearly living in a post-human age. What's human about Pol Pot and his killing fields? What's human about ex-Yugoslavia? Ex-Yugoslavia is peopled by ex-humans, the slaughtered and the slaughterers alike. How does that suit your fixed ideas? I think your fixed ideas need fixing."

"You know what you are?" asked Jacob.

"No. What am I?" replied Esau.

"You're a nut. A dangerous nut."

"You know what you are?" asked Esau.

"No. What am I?" replied Jacob.

"You're a sellout. You've sold out to the Greeks and their top down, slavemaster, aristocratic mentality that proceeds in terms of imposed ideas. Ideas from on high being the real thing and everything else being imitation. It never occurs to them, because it's never been to their advantage for it to occur to them, that what they call imitation is the real thing."

"The trouble with you," grumbled Jacob, "is you don't believe in the truth. Naturally, without the truth you can't have an imitation. That just means that everything and nothing is the truth. That's why you can take imitation for truth. Your truth is just fiction."

"No, you're wrong. I believe in truth, what I don't believe in is fiction. What you call fiction has lost its credibility. It's one of the dead ends of the Greco-Christian mentality, like the Immaculate Conception. You just have to remember that the truth comes in versions. I believe in the holy blessed version. Amen."

"Then who's to say your version is better than my version?"

"We argue."

"So what I call fiction you call a version?"

"I could call it a version, but I don't."

"What do you call it?"

"I call it narrative. Surprise."

"But I don't follow. Are you trying to tell me that narrative is a form of argument?"

"Exactly."

"What is there to argue over?"

"The truth."

"Oh no! I thought you just buried the truth."

"I only buried absolute truth. Narrative is the way we arrive at contingent truth."

"I thought that's what thinking does."

"Narrative is thinking. Story telling is a form of thinking. Our most common form of thinking. Even Plato used it to think about absolute truth. So do all the holy books. You think this is an accident maybe? The Bible, for example. The Bible is my bible."

"So narrative represents the truth."

"No. Narrative doesn't represent anything but itself."

"Okay, who's on first? Narrative is the truth but isn't the truth."

"Narrative is like talking. Is talking the truth? No, it's a way of getting at, adding to and communicating, among other things, what may be true while at the same time it's just—talk."

"Is what we're doing now narrative then?"

"It's dialogue, which as you know is a component of narrative, but an exemplary component. That is, it represents the basic argumentative nature of narrative, which is that if you aren't satisfied with my narrative, you trump it with your narrative."

"Where does it end then?"

"It doesn't. It's called living."

They were walking up hill out of the Valley of Gehenna and approaching the Jaffa Gate, through which they could already glimpse the Old City of Jerusalem.

"You know what you are?" asked Jacob.

"No. What am I?" replied Esau.

"A cynic."

"No, not a cynic. But a sophist, maybe, though sophists have a bad rep, thanks to Plato. As do poets, meaning artists of any kind. You know why?"

"Why?"

"Because artists, like sophists, know how to change their minds. To keep up with experience. And they know how to change your mind. That's why Plato thought they were dangerous. And they are. Plato knew that, because he was a great artist. That's why he won his argument with the Sophists about absolute truth, and that's why his ideas about imitation of reality became dominant in the Greco-European tradition. That's why we have come to believe that artists of all kinds are purveyors of beauty, not truth. That's why what we call fiction, though it's only existed for two hundred years, is considered our basic narrative form, denying the existence of a much older tradition of narrative which, when recognized, will crush the whole concept of fiction like the flimsy butterfly it is. And let's not forget either, brother, that we are not Greeks but Jews. And that the Ten Commandments explicitly and severely forbid any sort of imitation, under the rubric of 'graven images.' And that the basic books of our Western tradition are, after all, not Plato's, but the books of the Bible. No matter how artful Plato's *Dialogues* are."

"Plato, I beg to differ, was not interested in beauty but truth."

"Beauty doesn't even exist. Beauty is just truth after the fact. That's the reason that Keats could say beauty is truth, truth beauty. It all depends on when you look."

They were now entering the Old City of Jerusalem, the point of departure and the destination of many great truths. Once through the Jaffa Gate they stared about, as they did each time they entered the walled city, in awe.

"Beautiful, isn't it," said Jacob.

"Gorgeous."

Chat

A château in France, a velveteen covered desk, a soft changing light in the salon on a day of rolling whites and wispy greys with sunny *éclaircis*, a wall of glass doors through which little white butterflies playing tag over a flower dotted field. Early that morning he had seen a goshhawk, a black kite, and various song birds in the chateau forest as well as three grey herons at a piece of water on the property in the Val de Loire. He was listening to the meditations of a Schubert quintet, C major, D956 (op. 163), the Weller Quartet with Dietfried Gurtler second cello. In the final movement, dance-like, the butterflies seemed to be dancing in the air to Schubert.

"Cowly owl, is it not?" remarked his companion in French, a Frenchman.

"Very owl," Waldo affirmed. Waldo did not understand French very well, he was in the habit of translating conversation, often a little too literally, as it unfolded. In the case of *vachement chouette*, since *vache* meant cow, *vachement* must have meant cowly, while *chouette* meant screech owl. He assumed his companion was talking about the view, which looked like a tapestry, but why a tapestry should look like an owl, much less a cow, he couldn't tell. Maybe tapestries often had cows and owls in them, so that when a flowery field looked like a tapestry it was considered cowly owlish.

"The umbrellas are dancing to the music," Pierre went on. This one stopped Waldo until he remembered that he often got *parapluie* mixed up with *papillon*, butterfly.

"You noticed it also?" responded Waldo. "It is perhaps that one trains butterflies in France?" Lately he had been catching on to the custom of witty repartee here.

"I believe not," dry laugh. "We leave that and puritan sexual training to you Anglo-Saxons. It is rather that as the music plays the mind follows its rule, is it not?"

"But if the mind, as mine, does not understand the rules of music, how can it be otherwise than unruly?" asked Waldo.

"The rules of the game, my friend, do not need to be understood. Finally, one plays more easily by the rules when they are least understood," answered Pierre.

"Do we speak of playing? or gaming?" inquired Waldo. "Because while games have rules, play has none. The music may have rules but the mind can play with it as it wants."

"I am not in accord," said Pierre. "There are always rules, though we may not like them and at the limit they may be tragic. The first rule is death, and it is also the last. This is true, I believe, even in the United States."

"Yes, but for example," said Waldo. "American jazz has rules only in the making of it, so it is a kind of play to begin with. This is perhaps the case with all good music in some degree, that it discovers its rules finally in the process of composition, not before the fact. Thus the only ones who know the rules before the fact are the performers, and perhaps the audience. Then, for the players it is a game, while for the composer it is play."

"No doubt life is less complicated in the United States, but we have discovered that, in order to be liberated, you need rules to transgress, in order to be free you need first to be enchained. Read your Sade. All the same, we musn't forget either, my old person, that liberty is a French idea, and a French idea in the States is not the same as a French idea in France. But then, would you like to try a game of chess?" asked Pierre.

"Thank you, but I don't like games," replied Waldo. "I find them boring."

"Desolated. Then, till I see you again." Pierre left. There was a weekend party at the chateau with a various and international guest list. So, almost simultaneously, an American college student came in. Waldo was not excessively delighted at her entrance, since he was eager to be alone with Schubert and the dancing butterflies. And here was this rather plain and pious looking jeune-fille whose mind was no doubt seething with literal observations struggling to plod loose. But on second look she seemed to vibrate with a confusing if not confused energy and had a certain pneumatic fleshiness to her that cushioned the intrusion. She didn't say hello, what she said was, "Do you realize we're just a few kilometers from where Rabelais was born and raised?"

"You like Rabelais?" asked Waldo. A point in her favor.

"Give me a break! He was the best thing in my Humanities course. Rabelais is cool."

"What's so cool about Rabelais?" he inquired further.

"Because he'll just say anything," she exclaimed. "He's so experimental. He goes, like, completely loose."

"Saying you can just say anything is good example of saying anything. But you can't say anything, or you can but it can also be completely stupid," observed Waldo.

"What do you mean? I can say whatever I like. And I'm saying it."

"Really."

"Really. I'm an American. It's a free country. There aren't any rules on freedom of speech."

"Just because there are no rules doesn't mean you can say whatever you like. Let's take a walk," Waldo suggested.

He took her into the woods. It was late spring, the trees were full, the birds were out in force.

"What's your name? Jane?"

"How did you know?"

"You hear that, Jane?" Waldo said. "I mean the birdsong. You think they're just singing anything? They're singing to find mates, they're singing to define their territories. Experimental they are not. Nor are they playing games. But they are playing and their playing is a kind of thinking, thinking out loud, speaking your mind you might say if mind includes feelings as it indeed does, like a saxophone solo in a jazz piece. That's what Rabelais is like, a sax solo. Or maybe more like a raucous Dixieland band."

A crow flapped down, landing on a bough that bent under its weight. "If you want my opinion," said the crow, "you humans are very limited with your games and competitions. We crows have contests too, we often have flying contests, for example, but they're games that no one wins and no one loses. Your games are obsessed with death. Every game ends in a little death or an escape from death. The possibilities are very limited. You win or you lose. That's why your games are obsessive and repetitive, surrogate for death, the underlying rule. Very limited. While in our kind of play the possibilities are infinite and nurturing. Functional. Open ended, exploratory, a process of discovery, including exposure of hidden rules and discovery of new and better rules. As such it differs from games which impose their rules, creating an artificial situation cut off from reality and trapped in psychology. You can never escape from your obsessions and preconceptions."

"You do a lot of talking for a crow. What's your name?"

"Edgar Allen."

"I mean your last name."

"Crow."

"Ah. That explains your concern with death."

"It explains nothing. Just because Poe liked crows doesn't mean that crows like Poe. The favorite crow author is Laurence Sterne."

"Why is that?"

"He writes as the crow flies. The crow flies in zigs and zags, in spirals and swoops, in grand detours and flappy fractals, but always finds the shortest vector between two points."

"The falcon is faster and more direct."

"Ah, but those are different kinds of points. They only factor speed and direction. Which is not the point. The point is you have to remember that crows are animals, despite their great intelligence. And that beside that the intelligence of animals is in some ways more acute than the intelligence of people. Only we express it differently. Birds, for example, write with their bodies in the sky." He flapped his wings and jumped off his bough into the air, grazing tree trunks in his floppy flight.

"You talk to crows?" exclaimed Jane incredulously.

"I talk to whoever listens. I talk to you. I talk to the dead."

"But do they answer?"

"Of course. When asked. Where would we be if the dead didn't answer? Gnawing on bones in caves."

"I'm a vegetarian," she objected.

"On carrots, then. Don't be too literal, it confuses me."

"What were you talking about? With the crow?"

"We were talking about mistaken ideas of form."

"What do you mean by form?"

"What do I mean by form? You're absolutely Socratic, do you know that? Next you'll be asking me what I mean by mean."

Jane looked upset. "I'm sorry, I didn't intend to be Socratic. I'll try to be less Socratic but I don't even know what you mean exactly."

"Let's say that form is your footprints in the sand. Do you understand footprints in the sand?"

"Yes, but . . ."

"Then you understand form."

"But I . . ."

"Believe me that's all you need to understand. Now you can forget it."

"Give me an example."

"The best example I can think of is a writer named Ronald Sukenick."

"Oh, right. We had to read him in my Postmodern Fiction course. He really turned me off."

"Oh really."

"Really. I couldn't understand what he was talking about."

"He was talking about you. No doubt that's why you couldn't understand him."

"Well why is he a good example of form?"

"Of a certain kind of form. The kind of form that informs everyday life. Not the kind of form frozen in great examples from the past."

"I still don't understand."

"No. And the fish doesn't understand water."

"Sukenick's book wasn't even writing. It didn't have plot or characters or a message."

"Which one did you read?"

"*Long Talking Bad Conditions Blues.*"

"That's one of the best examples of the kind of formal organization implicit in contemporary life."

"Why?"

"Why, why. Because it employs fractal organization, discontinuity, interactivity, ellipse, eclipse, non-sequitur, incompletion, association, chance, coincidence, achronicity, synchronicity, improvisation, intervention, self-contradiction, overlap, mosaic, modularity, graphic composition, sonic formation, rhythmic symmetry, vortextualization and eddyfication, rhizomatic interconnection, hypertextual hopscotch, paradox, wordplay, and in conclusion, inconclusion, all of it fluctuating faster than thought. Just look around you."

"All I can see is trees.

"That's why you don't see the forest."

"I mean all that stuff you're talking about, I never heard of it."

"Complain to your professors. Nobody ever heard of it in 1979 either, when Sukenick wrote it."

"Unless you mean, like, Tom Robbins. He's really cool."

"Get out of here."

"What do you mean?"

"I mean beat it."

"But I don't know where I am."

"Good. Get lost, Jane. That's exactly what you need."

He left her standing there, mouth open as if to say something which, luckily, he would never have to hear.

Quickly wheeling into an intersecting path, Waldo almost bumped into a ruddy man with big belly, blue blazer, greying beard, and stick, topped by a yachting cap, all of it very naval.

"I say, what's the rush?" An Englishman obviously.

"I'm fleeing Generation X. Aren't you?"

"Can one? Horatio," thrusting out his hand.

"No. Waldo," taking it.

"I say, was that you reeling off that impressive list of terminology that I heard through the trees?"

"That depends on who wants to know."

"What I mean, old boy, is it takes me back to the old days at Eton and Oxbridge."

"How so?"

"Because what they used to do was whip us into remembering long lists of rhetorical terms. And what was wafting through the trees, though I couldn't hear it too distinctly, sounded suspiciously like a long list of rhetorical terms."

"I didn't think of it that way."

"You should do a glossary, old boy."

"Somebody should, not me. But I suppose you have a point."

"Of course I have a point. If I didn't have a point I would have bloody well kept my mouth shut. My point is that you Yanks always think you're being original when you're just repeating something that's been done before and done better. You're almost as bad as the bloody Frogs who can't do anything without making a bloody revolution out of it."

"It may be true that I'm talking a new kind of rhetoric, at least you could look at it that way. And it may even be true that the whole deconstructive movement in letters consists of a rediscovery of rhetoric after a long period of lost prestige, one that parallels a loss of prestige for representation and perspective in painting. But there's one big difference in my connection to the tradition, and that is it's strictly antiformalist. Maybe because I'm American."

"There's no such thing as American, old boy. Maybe it's because you're colonial would be more like it. Postcolonialism is the dirty secret of American so-called culture. Despite the fact we're currently being over run by the tide of populist sewage generated by your consumer economy. Though I have to admit it's not as bad as the potential injection of continental influences through the bloody Common Market. We've already had our first case of rabies in a hundred years, no doubt the result of some mad dog racing through the bloody Chunnel."

"It's true that in the States we have a schizzy view of the ex-colonizing nations, France no less than England—favoring one over the other with excessive respect combined with excessive contempt—or maybe just plain excess of affect. We're a schizoid culture. Our formative catastrophes, the Revolutionary and Civil wars, were each in their ways schizophrenic. In European cultures the major threat comes from outside, encouraging paranoia. And as everyone knows, paranoia is a powerful way of organizing experience in fixed systems. Thus the great surrogate universes of Modernist art, basically a European movement, in which the important American influences lead straight to Postmodernism. Leaving aside Tom Pynchon, who with his paranoid style is maybe our most Modernist writer."

"And what has this got to do with antiformalism, pray?"

"Because schizophrenia is a fluctuating system. It keeps changing perspectives and doesn't tolerate fixed form. It breaks down virtuosity, that necessary complement of formalism, the talent of repeating a single mode better than anyone else. As opposed to improvisation, the ability to invent new modes so that perfection of them becomes secondary. The net result is a democratization of culture and its expression in the arts. You don't need to sing a high C better than anyone else, that's not the point."

"My god, it sounds as if all this adds up to some sort of nouveau populism. We don't want any more little Ezra Pounds running around, do we?"

"One thing is that in the States the outsider tactic of the so-called avant-garde may have always been based on an ill-conceived imitation of European models. That was one of Pound's first mistakes—damn the man in the street. In America the outside becomes the 'in' side with amazing rapidity. So much so that the best path to advancement in the American arts is to present yourself as a rebel. What it adds up to is that change in the States comes from inside not outside. Everyone in the States instinctively realizes this. Henry Miller is just an extension of the born again strain in American culture. Salvation in rebirth, not in social welfare or political programs. Though a politician who embodies that hope of personal regeneration will make a clean sweep. In the States the personal is the best way to gain media access to the public. That's because public space is wiping out personal space, making it available only in public."

"It seems to me that anyone caught up in the American media machine will just be ground up and spit out in the image of the consumerist status quo."

"Anyway, there's no choice. There is no outside any more. Electronics have done away with that kind of spatial metaphor, and even temporal conceptions essential to an avant-garde movement have been annulled in the electrosphere. On the Internet it doesn't matter where you are or when you are."

"Are we speaking of selling out here?"

"There are some things that can't be sold because they can't be bought. No, we're talking about mutiny. If I were a politican I'd propose a platform of progressive mutiny. Mutiny does not need a program, it does not need an ideology. Mutiny is not revolution or even rebellion. It does not need leaders and it does not need blood. It does not proceed from alienation, but is an impulse from the inside to reclaim its own identity. It is an eruption of the spiritual unconscious. Mutiny is a movement of collective conviction and revulsion, a refusal to proceed as usual, a diversion of the channels of power to more constructive ends. A mutiny does not even have to win and so can't be defeated. There's nothing to win, there's simply the diffusion of a vision as the agent of change. Currently it's the Internet versus the world wide cobweb. 1968 was a mutiny that changed Western culture more profoundly than a revolution. In comparison, the Russian Revolution was an upheaval that turned

Russia into, well, Russia. The Civil Rights Movement was a mutiny. The fall of the Iron Curtain was a mutiny. The ecological movement is a mutiny in progress."

"Not to my way of thinking. Mutiny is just a symptom of *nostalgie de la boue*, as they say here, and the kind of people who have that impulse are no better than swine rooting in mud."

"There are more ways of thinking, Horatio, than are defined in the Trivium and Quadrivium. Not to mention Wittgenstein's *Tractatus*."

"I like the ways of thinking we already have, thank you. Introducing others can only cause trouble. Who knows what people might start thinking about?"

"What I'm talking about is quite practical really. You English are supposed to be good at that. I'm simply saying that the forms of culture we have to work with don't work and that the only kind of form worth talking about today is form that's completely eccentric. You're supposed to be good at that too. Being eccentric."

"What does eccentric mean to you?"

"Doing something the wrong way that turns out to be right."

"Now why would that make any sense at all?"

"Because there is no right way. Trying to do something the right way, therefore, is precisely when you go wrong. Never rule out the unacceptable. Coming at things with no preconceptions is the way, but you only know it's right after the fact. That's why Art Brut is so interesting, because it's by definition beyond the acceptable. There's only one thing that's totally and finally unacceptable in art and that is art itself, the category and all the institutions that support it. It's industrial culture's way of isolating a number of powerful human faculties that aren't productive in it, that may even be disruptive for it. Museums, libraries, campuses are actually zoos within the game preserve of what we call culture. In fact Art Brut isn't art, it's a prison break."

"Of course I've heard of Art Brut, but my impression is that it's simply work by autodidacts, convicts, and crazies without any criteria. People who should probably be loaded on a lorry and dumped in the Loire."

"But that's the thing, there are no artistic criteria, there are just the criteria of everyday life—intellect, spirit, information, relevance, utility, elegance, perception, etcetera. What's wrong with that? Those are the criteria we should be applying anyway. The same ones we apply to any craft or intellectual pursuit. Special criteria make the arts into a power trip, irrelevant and impotent, except as another way for so-called experts to bully people who aren't in on the game."

"Well, I mean, you need something to bully people with, after all, and art seems a good solution. Obviously you don't want to use a machine gun when you can use a fire hose. Let's try to be humane."

"You're interested in domination, I'm interested in liberation."

"I hope you know what you're in for when you start liberating people."

"Whatever it is in we're in for we're in for anyway because people have already been programmed for domination and submission. But I'm a deprogrammer, that's how I get my kicks."

"So when you don't like a program you just give it a kick and hope for the best?"

"No, I start with the little things. How to read. How to write. How to think."

"Is there a method to this madness?"

"You have to go back to what you call my rhetoric. It all adds up to reader liberation."

The trees were thinning out and opening up. Soon they came in sight of the old château.

"Well," remarked Waldo, "looks like we're out of the woods."

"I think it'll be a while," replied Horatio, "before you're out of the woods, old chap. Pardon me, we're getting toward lunch, or at least I am." He headed for the château, while Waldo stretched out on a canvas trans-at, admiring the well-kept elegance of the grounds as well as the buildings themselves. They must require a lot of attention. Who was responsible for all this? Waldo wondered, as the old Châtelaine appeared on a terrace, framed by a gothic doorway, in her gardening clothes smoking her pipe.

"Hurr," said a rather feline voice. Waldo looked around but didn't see anybody in his immediate vicinity.

"Hurr, hurr," the voice again. It seemed to be coming from somewhere close, maybe even from his own body. He felt a subtle pressure through the canvas of his chair against his butt and looking down, saw that a large cat was raising its rump to stretch against the bottom of the trans-at. It was a grey on grey tiger striped cat looking very male, and when Waldo put his hand down to caress it it came out from under the chair with a loud growling meow.

"Hurr," said the cat.

"Her," repeated Waldo. "So you think she's the one who attends to everything so well here? Well I guess you're right, since she's the boss."

"Rararow," said the cat, rubbing its ear against Waldo's leg.

"Yes," said Waldo. "Three cheers is right, seeing the attention she obviously gives to every detail. There's something admirable in that."

"Murrah."

"Yes, even morally admirable. Because of the intellectual rigor involved."

"Wharaoww, wharrr, row."

"Why intellectually rigorous? Well, you know her better than I do, what do you think?" Waldo scratched its head, and it responded by rubbing it against his hand while purring, as if to communicate secrets.

"Ah! So you think she has a gift for attention. You think that attention is the key. You think that most humans don't have the gift for concentration that almost all cats have. The ability to focus on something and really examine it, probe all its possibilities and even go further to meditate on it with all sentient faculties including seeing hearing feeling smelling tasting and whiskers, all which properly activated belong to a full definition of intellect. You believe that the inability to concentrate is the source of the Freudian idea of repression, which essentially comes out of a diversion of attention from something uncomfortable to think about. So that this is all about levels of attention, you think, a notion which is not at all confined to psychology but to media manipulation, politics, economics, love, and the spiritual dimension of the self which cats are in touch with in an eminently practical way but which humans tend to ignore as too intangible to count for much. So it all comes down to levels of attention, you think, and everything else is bullshit. And you think that some humans nevertheless are in touch with the gift of attention of which you speak? And they are called writers, artists, musicans, and the like, but that they are only in touch in a sadly fragmented and rudimentary way and are focused, like scholars or stock brokers, on their little specialties?"

"Yaoouw."

"Well I agree with almost everything you say. Except that I think that artists of any kind who are really good are fully in touch with these faculties, exploring and preserving them for the rest of a mentally crippled humankind until such time as it might awaken to the possibilities of a broader, more effacacious, and more generous consciousness."

"Wowou."

"Wow is right. You take my breath away. Of all the folks I've talked to this morning you're the only one who seems very sensible."

"Mrarrr-r-r."

"You're welcome."

Much to Waldo's surprise, since he was concentrating on his conversation with the cat, the Châtelaine was now standing over his trans-at, her distinguished wrinkles wrinkled with another set of intensely quizzical ones.

"Talking to my cat?" she asked, removing her little pipe from her mouth, the pipe a small sign of her eccentric sense of order. "I'm sure you'll find him quite reasonable."

"Oh I do. We've had a long and interesting conversation."

"About what?"

"About philosophy."

"Truly. He talks with me mostly about food. But, you know, we French, like the Italians, like to talk about food. Speaking of which, lunch is ready."

"Well," said Waldo, "I'd like to chat with him again sometime. What's his name?"

"Chat."

A la Bastille

(Get Drunk, Drive Fast)

They were walking across the tree-shaded ivy-trimmed grass-carpeted patch of privilege known as a campus, continuing the discussion that had begun in the Professor's office.

"Assuming it's true," hemmed the Professor, "what you're arguing, that there are no outsiders any more . . ."

"Not so much no outsiders as no outside," corrected Waldo. "You used to be able to exist quite comfortably outside. With a sense of superiority even. You were practically smug about being left out, proud of being attacked by the establishment, it was part of the identity. Now if you're outside you simply don't exist. Because there is no outside. And as soon as your exclusion is noticed, or as soon as you're attacked for not being inside, you are inside. You exist. It's good to be discovered as alternative or transgressive, it's even better to be attacked. It's convertible into dollars. Howard Stern, for example."

"An unfortunate example," said the Professor, absently. "But I assume there are still sides of some sort, even if not in and out."

"Oh, there are sides, I suppose there's even a history of sides. Yours begins with the entry of the Vietnam generation into the Ph.D. mill, I believe," Waldo said vaguely. This wasn't a very interesting discussion and besides, he was busy eyeballing the passing nubility. The campus was aswarm with eminently harassable young women and strapping boys emitting almost tangible hormones. As an occasional young adjunct instructor, Waldo thanked god he had been missed by the local autocastration indoctrination squads.

"That's right," said the Professor. "And history, before it ended, went as follows." The Professor was a founding member of AADD, Academics Against Decadent Deconstruction, but he wasn't really paying attention because he was thinking about a conference he had just been invited to at the Club Med in French Samoa. Though by now he was able to deliver the party line by rote.

"It was a generation that was peeved with America, and looked to Paris, which at the time was known for its independence from, if not contempt for, the U.S. as the black hole of Western culture. Young American academics were delighted with a new perspective reenforcing a habitual tweedy bossiness long frayed by apparent irrelevance. But it turned out that Boss Tweed was no more immune to fame and fortune than the rest of us. The academic stars from abroad flocked to America for their fifteen minutes, not to mention lucrative lecture fees and textbook sales. Their domestic avatars were soon bragging about high salaries that put them in the income bracket of minor CEOs. Academics of a Marxist persuasion were quick to jump on the Brinks truck. After all, they knew how to play the realpolitik game. Professors of oppressed minorities versed in the new terminology also proved excellect practitioners of Brinksmanship. Excluded women academics who talked the talk were among the first at the trough. The canon exploded—what was in was out and what was out was in. Students were reading books undeservedly ignored and were undeservedly ignorant of books formerly prominent. Did it make any difference? Sure it did—to those who got seats on the gravy train."

Waldo wasn't taking much of this in. As a regular reader of *The Nation* he wasn't about to buy the point of view of a confirmed Neocon. Instead he was plotting micropolitics with miniskirts. His favorite thing was to methodically seduce as many of the coeds in his classes as possible, the better to politicize them. It was one of the advantages of being a low paid, no-benefit academic temp. Besides, he could double dip by using the seduction adventures in writing pornography to supplement his income. He also liked to get drunk and drive fast.

"Let me pass on to you," said the Professor, "some academic advice from a distinguished professor of the Old Left given to me as a then novice Neocon. He said, 'Never mind about creative achievement. You publish your book, you get your student claque, you hike your salary with competing job offers every chance you get. Then you can worry about achievement.' So you see, it doesn't matter whether you're left or right, you play the same game."

"That's cynical," said Waldo.

"Dear me," replied the Professor. "There may, or may not, be two sides. Those with steady incomes and those without. It's a matter of situation. An old anarcho-socialist writer I know, committed to that point of view since he was a teenager, finally had a best seller at the age of fifty-five. First thing he did was to write an article for *The Nation* declaring the end of socialism."

"Anyway," said Waldo, "I teach Creative Writing, so I'm not a party to this racket."

"Creative Writing, exclamation point," said the Professor. "Creative Writers are the worst. Scratch a poet and a redneck will say ouch. An intellectual redneck, that is. Though novelists are worse than poets. Poets have to claim a certain amount of expertise—novelists take pride in operating out of ignorance."

"Do I detect a lack of sympathy with the arts?"

"On the contrary. We Neocons may like the good old stuff, but at least we like it. At least we recognize that culture is the matrix for politics. That's why we always win the culture wars, we're the only ones interested in winning them. The Lefties always harbor a secret contempt for the arts, because they see them as mystifications of real social issues. There's nothing so disastrous as a leftist academic theorist in face of a poem, because the theorists have forgotten how to think about poetry and the leftists don't want to. Anyway, that's my theory."

"It's practice, not theory, that will save the world," said Waldo.

"Nothing will save the world," said the Professor.

They had now reached the edge of the scholastic greensward and were crossing into the benighted city—cars, pollution, noise, garbage cans, dog shit, convenience shops, mini-malls, megastores, bad tempers, cross-purposes, hurry, worry, guarded regards, extravagant graffiti.

"Okay, Professor," said Waldo, "why are we here?"

"I have a proposal," said the Professor. "I control the purse strings of a certain academic resource, what the vulgar might term a slush fund, in short. And I gather you're a little strapped for cash." He looked up inquiringly.

"Always," responded Waldo.

"The grad assistants and adjuncts are starting a union," the Professor non sequitured.

"So?"

"I'd like you to join it."

"Why?"

"Because a union would be inconvenient. Our whole system depends on underpaying teaching assistants."

"So you want to play hardball?" asked Waldo.

"We couldn't help notice that you weren't very sympathetic to the ideology of the organizers."

"That's just because I'm not very sympathetic to anything," explained Waldo. "Doctrine is always baloney."

"And of course you'd become my assistant," said the Professor. "With a guaranteed teaching load."

"It's not that I have any objection to being an administration fink. It's just I don't think we speak the same language," said Waldo.

"What language do you speak?"

"The same language as these grafitti around us. The nonspecific language of universal discontent."

"That sounds very literary," said the Professor.

"When you say the word literature you pull your rank. Literature is just a classy name for a class domination game. Don't forget I work for a book chain. I sell literature."

"Which book chain?" asked the Professor.

"Swarms Ignoble. So I know what literature is. It's a money laundering scheme."

"How so?"

"Because it doesn't sell," said Waldo.

"Then what are all those literary books doing there?"

"Wallpaper," said Waldo. "They need something to put on the shelves. That's why book returns to publishers are going up over fifty percent."

"So what do they sell?"

"Nothing," said Waldo. "Coffee maybe."

"Then why are they opening more and more stores?" asked the Professor. "They must be making money."

"Sales go up profits go down. They operate in the red. You know the old garment industry joke? How do you make a profit if you lose a dollar on every suit you sell? Answer: Volume!"

"You shock me," said the Professor. "I'm genuinely shocked. Surely literature must be more than this."

"What you call literature could be more than this," replied Waldo, "if our critics and academics were capable of subtracting market force from intellectual force in given works, market force in this case equalling form. Only then will you get a literature that frees readers to participate in the realization of the work rather than constraining them to submit to a variety of hypnosis. Also known as willing suspension of disbelief, a ploy based on consensual domination and submission. To deformalize in our socioeconomic context means to deprogram, and deprogramming means reader liberation. So you get them where it counts, in how they read and write and, therefore, think."

"Surely you're not an antiformalist?" queried the Professor.

"Form is your foot prints in the sand," responded Waldo.

"So what's the point?" asked the Professor.

"The point is that literature is a money laundering scheme. Just like museums and symphony orchestras. Like the opera. Fine art. Ballet. Even jazz clubs. Mostly they don't make a profit—they're money losers. Thank god for the Mafia and the Robber Barons. Thank god for the drug cartels. The NEA was just a side show."

"Can you prove this?"

"If I could prove it I'd be dead. Or worse, accused of bad taste."

"Maybe we speak the same language after all," said the Professor. "We Neocons know, though we don't tell anyone, that taste is always formed by three things. Money, sex, and politics. None of them ever admitted. They're part of the cultural unconscious. Abstract Expressionism got off the ground because the State Department decided it'd be good propaganda for the American Century. The Beatniks suddenly found themselves headlined in Hearst publications because they were used to signal the shift from a puritan work economy to a hedonist consumer economy. Jerzy Kosinski, who as all but literary morons know couldn't write his way out of a paper bag without massive help, bamboozled the New York intelligentsia, left and right, with his peculiar concoction of sex and politics until the *New York Times Sunday Magazine* went too far by publishing an outrageous S & M photo of him on its cover."

"This is getting interesting," said Waldo. "What do you say we go over to the Swarms Ignoble and coffee stain some books and magazines?"

Over at the Superstore, the Professor waved his hand at the Babel of books around them. "You see this surplus of choice?" he said. "This is free market democracy."

"Anyone in the book business can tell you," replied Waldo, "that almost all the books here are produced by a handful of publishers that have cannibalized all the other publishers, and are themselves owned by a teaspoonful of international conglomerates that dominate the entertainment and communication business worldwide. So if you think that Rupert Murdoch and Si Newhouse have the best interests of democracy at heart you'll continue to sleep soundly."

"But surely," said the Professor, "you can find anything you want here."

"Sure you can. If you know about it. But you won't know about it because it's not a matter of the physical 'product,' as they call books in the publishing world, it's a matter of attention. And at best your attention will be directed toward skillful but harmless practitioners like Philip Roth and John Updike. Or at the GenX limit, Tom Robbins. Books that contain what I call a negative political component based not on what's included but on what isn't. The cultural unconscious is a composed of what's left out and therefore doesn't exist. Now if there were some smart critics around they'd begin probing that unconscious. But I'm not holding my breath."

"We academics are concerned with deeper issues," smugged the Professor.

"Maybe," said Waldo. "But any contemporary literary analysis that doesn't begin with some consideration of the influence of the late capitalist institutions that produce the books you read—and write— is worse than foolish. Come to think, maybe it's because they produce the books you write that you prefer to think about deeper issues."

"This is getting personal."

"It should. Because the literary-industrial complex that dominates the so-called Humanities is controlled by persons, and you may be one of them. An unconscious lackey, as they used to call them, of the ruling class, as they used to call it."

"What makes you say 'unconscious'?" asked the Professor. "We Neocons were not born yesterday."

"Hey, maybe we are on the same wave length. I think I'll take you up on that proposition. I've always been a union sympathizer. Solid aridity forever!"

"Are we talking maybe coalition politics here?" asked the Professor.

"No. Unless it's the coalition of mutineers against orthodoxies. Mutiny is my best bet because mutiny is immune to doctrine. A mutiny begins with individuals who are fed up, not with ideologies that are force-fed. A mutiny doesn't have a program so much as a set of grievances. Its aims beyond that are vague, but that very vagueness may be to its advantage, since beyond specific programs, it undermines the whole range of attitudes that produced the grievances in question. A mutiny is a moving target—because it has no set ideological objectives it mutates so quickly and unpredictably that it's hard to destroy. A mutiny mobilizes people of many differing political persuasions. Revolutions may begin with mutinies but revolutions either fail, or turn into mirrors of regimes they've destroyed, while the subterrenean effects of a mutiny on the culture may be enduring. The anti-Vietnam War movement was a mutiny, Paris in sixty-eight was a mutiny, the Civil Rights Movement was a mutiny. So, *à la Bastille!*"

Art Brute

LETTER TO THE EDITOR

Professors should have sex with their students and if they won't they should be fired. Sex is a powerful teaching tool, going back in our tradition to Socrates, and should not remain unexploited because of irrelevant moral concerns or limited energies on the part of professors. The professor's first obligation is to instruct, and excuses regarding time needed for research should cut no ice. The university has changed and demands accountability to the consumers who purchase its services, including especially the services of its teachers. That such a penetrating pedagogical implement should go unused, when it could plough untold fields that might otherwise lie fallow, is unconscionable at a time when demand for a quality educational product is at an unprecedented high.

Some may plead that senior professors be exempted from such duties, but this is outrageous. While it is true that instructors and graduate teaching assistants especially have maximal energy and enthusiasm for such tutorial projects, they have their own studies to pursue. Enough cynical exploitation of untenured faculty! This is a field in which everyone can make some contribution, and our students need contact with those demonstrating proven abilities and extensive vitas. We all need to fight in the trenches.

Let's look at the arguments involved in the harassment debate, con and pro. Why shouldn't students sleep with professors for grades? This is not a requirement that should be imposed on every student, to be sure, but those who are so inclined should not be denied the opportunity just because of the professor's disinclination.

Teaching is a job, after all, even though professors don't like to think of it that way. But look at it from the student's point of view: if you can't learn from your teacher in one way you should be able to learn in another. Many satisfied graduates look back to their faculty affairs as excellent learning experiences. Those professors who insist on leaving their office doors open during student conferences are not granting their clients their complete attention or their full resources.

In some circumstances, the professor may be the one to perceive that the student needs the closer relation that sex demands, while the latter does not yet realize it. To begin with, erotic affiliation is a good way to increase contact hours with any student. But whatever the need, the professor's judgment should be irrefutable in such cases. Careful evaluation of the situation must precede any action, but once the decision is made the professor must plunge in with a sure and experienced hand. Especially once contact is initiated, the student is not likely to be in a position to evaluate the benefits immediately or objectively. However, needless to say, studies should be undertaken to assess outcomes.

You may ask, How are professors going to handle these new burdens when they are already overworked and underpaid? The answer is that honoraria should be provided for faculty as an incentive. Some fair measure of compensation should be determined, either by the hour, the night, or the, well . . . head.

Waldo pushed his laptop back, let loose a sigh, reflecting that every time he tried to exploit his talent as a writer for immediate worldly gain it backfired. Why was that? Maybe it was because whenever he started writing he never knew where he was going to end up. Out of control. Usually it wasn't where he thought he would end up. He picked up the phone. Dialed a number, heard it ring two, three times, then Newt's voice: "Hello?"

Newt was a leftist friend of his who did Marxist theory which he put to good use in the micropolitics of what he called ackpol, a.k.a. academic politics.

"Hi, it's Waldo. I finished, but you're not going to like it."

"Why not?"

"I started thinking about it . . ."

"Who told you to start thinking about it?"

"I couldn't help it. And it came out with a somewhat different spin from what we were talking about."

"How did that happen?"

"Well, you want to get this guy fired, right? For screwing his student, right?"

"Right."

"Well what got me thinking was you married one of your students, right? And when you started going out with her she was in one of your freshman classes, right? And you were about forty-five, right? And it's a very good marriage, right?"

"Damn right. But what's that got to do with it? I could have met her anywhere, it just happened to be in class. And we just happened to get along. And besides, she was the one who started flirting with me."

"Then I remembered you also told me once that you were seduced by your French professor as an undergraduate. And that your fluency improved by leaps and bounds."

"It's true my accent improved. But what's good for me isn't necessarily good for other people. We have to protect our students from exploitation. And we have to protect our professors from themselves."

"We should start a teacher's union. We could get together and protect one another from ourselves with a united front."

"Were you counting on teaching here again next semester?"

"Yeah why?"

"Just asking. We may be old friends but there are professional limits."

The hint did not go unnoticed. Waldo was an academic temp. He taught courses here and there and it wasn't even his main job. He didn't have a main job. He was a part-time professor, a part-time high school sub, a part-time researcher, a part-time investigator, a part-time bartender, a part-time cab driver, a part-time dope dealer. Whatever. Whatever it took to make a living. Something he had been trying to do and not quite succeeding at for a number of years. Things had gone from worse to awful lately since his girlfriend had left for a teaching job in Missoula, Montana, without inviting him along, because she'd been providing most of the household income. Anyway, he wouldn't have gone along. His several excursions out of what he referred to as Manahatt had not been great personal successes. Four years in the Gallic precincts of the Ivy League getting educated had left him with an allergy to French culture that required another four years in a more traditional California graduate school for reconstruction. But he found he was already too deconstructed to get it together. A victim of deleuzions, he considered himself "rhizomatic," that is, much like a potato. And much like a potato he did nothing to finish his degree. Deciding that there was something in the air of Manahatt that he needed for survival, he decided to go back for good.

Stay put at all costs was his current plan. There was a problem though. His landlord, Slumski, claimed that his girlfriend was the lawful tenant in the apartment and that he, Waldo, was illegally subletting. He was using this ploy to get him off rent control, which would mean Slumski could charge whatever he wanted and Waldo would have to move out. That would mean he'd have to leave Manahatt because he'd never find another place he could afford. Maybe he could get the roaches to pay the rent. They were the real tenants of the apartment whoever lived there.

It was time to go out. There was a nude multisexual poetry slam at the Pyramid Club he wanted to catch. But first he had to feed the roaches. He knew from experience that he couldn't get rid of them, so as soon as his girlfriend left for the boonies he initiated what he called the Waldoplan. The idea was to feed the roaches before you go out. Feed them as much as they want, feed them more than they can eat. They really don't eat that much, when you think about it, compared to a human, like himself. Or compared to a polar bear, which he might not be able to support, though which he might in some ways prefer. But for himself and the roaches there was enough. By the time he got back they would be satiated and sleeping happily in their burrows, or where ever they slept. He didn't care, as long as they didn't bother him. You could not beat Manahatt, you could only accommodate to it.

There were a lot of things you couldn't beat these days, more than there used to be. The Beat Generation had it easy by comparison. They could drop out. Actually, the Beats were among the first dropouts to get picked up by the media. But not right away. Now, the instant you dropped out you were picked up by the media. And once you dropped out you could drop back in. You could drop out for the evening and drop back in for work the next morning. You could even drop out for a few hours and then drop back in, maybe even for a few minutes. He suspected the truth was there was really nothing to drop out to any more, so dropping out just had the effect of making you more in.

He'd read about the nude multisexual poetry slam in the *New York Times*. The media was one of the things you couldn't beat, you could only use it, be used by it, or be ignored by it. He'd even gone to the trouble of making a list of things you couldn't beat. It was the beginning of what he called a fractal list in which each item could itself become the idea behind another list that could give rise to a parallel set of items each of which could become the idea for similar lists till things that first appeared in one list would start overlapping other lists developing subtle and complex interconnections.

Things you couldn't beat:

1. City Hall
1. Wall Street
1. Multinational conglomerates
1. Intelligence agencies
1. Drug cartels
1. Money
1. Poverty
1. Death
1. Disorder
1. Chance

Which brings up the question of order, that is, why number a set of ten things from one to one instead of a series of things from one to ten. Answer: it's simply one sort of order among many. All things swim and glitter. Once we lived in what we saw. Now, in a quantum world where microphenomena can be two or more places at once or even two or more different things at once or even during two or more times at once we certainly need to entertain the possibility of more than one kind of order if we're going to be in touch with the way things are. It all depends on how you're looking at things, which depends on what you need to look at. Which requires keeping on your toes. Our love of the real draws us to permanence, but as health depends on circulation, sanity depends on variety and facility of perception. Dedication to one version of the real is quickly odious, if not dangerous. Life is a series of surprises, and the only way to keep up with it is by spontaneity and improvisation. Implying, of course, a corresponding antiformalist art of nonsequitur, discontinuity, and incompletion. This requires an ability to live in the instant so as to scope out the immediate content of real time. There are moments when we all loosen the bonds of memory that govern the way we usually think for the sake of increased responsiveness to the present. He'd read somewhere recently that such a focus actually makes use of a special part of the brain. If so, experience tells him that this is the part of the brain that writers and artists depend on, and probably also basketball players, musicans, magicians, children, animals, and anyone else whose occupation demands that you function faster than you normally think. It also helps explain the improbable antagonism between intellectuals and artists. Intellectuals have more memory, artists have faster modems. Their attention focuses on different phenomena.

It was raining when he went out. He decided to take a cab but he knew this was one of those situations you couldn't beat—if the weather was good you didn't want a cab, if it was bad you couldn't get one. But he also knew that situations you couldn't beat sometimes beat one another, leaving chance openings for anyone nimble enough to slip through. It was eleven at night. The streets were empty, few people few cars, the rain falling lightly but whipped by a mean wind. He walked up to Fourteenth Street, took shelter in a doorway and waited.

Soon he saw a young woman walking down First Avenue dressed in a stylish pants suit with no raincoat trying to hold up a rather dainty flowered umbrella in the wind while talking into a cell phone and with the same arm carrying an attache case. When she saw him in the doorway she stopped talking and came over.

"Where am I?" she asked.

"Excuse me?" He saw that she was Asian.

"Which way is the Wardolf Astolia?"

Waldo was probably the only person in Manahatt who didn't know where the Waldorf Astoria was, but he knew it wasn't on First Avenue. He pointed crosstown. "Somewhere that way."

"Wait a minute," into the phone. To him, "You mean you don't know where is the Wardolf Astolia?"

"Are you staying there?"

"No, I'm thinking of buying it."

"Listen, you don't have to be sarcastic." He was a little offended.

Into the phone, "He doesn't bereave . . . He doesn't know where . . . There is no one erse." To him, "Is this Pok Avenue?"

"This is First Avenue and Fourteenth Street."

Into the phone, "Filst Avenue and Fawlteen Stleet . . . That orlight, they can show it me tomollow molning befaw the meeting . . . Send it here, I wait." She hung up. "Thanks faw yaw herp," she said, but she didn't go anywhere. Neither did he. Finally, "Why did you say that?" he asked.

"What?"

"About the hotel."

"Because it tloo. My company sent a team here to see if they can buy it. I the intelpletaw."

"Where are you from?"

"Tokyo. But I have a deglee in Amelican Ritalatcha."

"Really. That's what I teach. What's your specialty?"

"Larf Wardo Emelson. I can quote him by halt. 'Or things swim and grittaw. Once we rivved in what we saw. Our rove of the lear dlaws us to pelmanence, but as hearth depends on circuration, sanity depends on valiety and facirity of pelception. Dedication to one velsion of the lear is quickry odious, if not dangelous. Rife is a selies of sulplises, and the onry way to keep up with it is by spontaneity and implovisation.' That's flom the essay 'Expelience,' but I plobabry sclewed it up a ritter."

"I don't remember that one, though I probably read it some time or other."

"I'm shaw evly Amelican lead it. Here comes my ca."

A ridiculously long white limo pulled up and a chauffer with a cap jumped out and opened a door. She looked over her shoulder as she got in. "I can give you a lide somewhea?"

"Sure." He'd actually walked away from the Pyramid Club in his effort to get there because it was easier to get a cab on Fourteenth Street. Now walking there in the rain was out of the question. But as he gave the driver the address he reflected that sometimes you had to go in the opposite direction to get where you wanted to go. In any case, that was his habitual tack, though some people simply thought he didn't know where he was going. His reasoning was that sometimes where you were going wasn't where it was supposed to be, or if it was, you couldn't get there from here. But the real reason was he didn't like to know where he was going. In the long run we're all going to one place so what's the rush? Nevertheless we're always in a hurry to get to our destinations, that seems to be the nature of the brute.

"I took a semesta in Okrahoma," she said as the limo pulled out, "but I neva been to New Yawk. I couldn't affawd to come. Now I can affawd evlything but I don't know what to do."

"Would you like to come to a nude multisexual poetry slam?"

"What is it?"

"I'm not even sure myself, I think you just have to see it to find out."

"Exprain a ritter. After or I have a deglee in Amelican Ritalatcha."

"You know the colloquialism it goes in one ear and out the other? Well, it's like that. Except in this case the ears belong to different people and it comes out of one and into the other."

"I don't undastand."

"What's your name?"

"Mieko."

"Waldo, pleased to meet you. So, Mieko, to begin at the beginning, once poetry was written on pages for people to read. Sometimes it still is. Then a Welsh poet named Dylan Thomas came along who was very good at reading poems out loud. He had, as we say, a wonderful ear, and even on the page his poems appealed mostly to the ear of the mind. Now many Americans don't like to read, and they especially don't like to read anything as complicated as poetry. But when Dylan Thomas read his poems out loud they didn't have to understand it they just had to hear it. Or maybe they understood but in a different way. This was very democratic because it could get poetry to a much bigger audience that didn't have a lot of the special education needed to read complicated poems on the page. Or, one might add, to write it. Later the same thing happened in art and in music with Pop Art and Punk Rock. And it was good because for example in poetry we now have two different kinds, the easy listening kind and the hard reading kind and people can take their choice of one or both or if they get interested in one sometimes they get interested in the other. It didn't begin as two different kinds and even now people mostly don't see that it's two different kinds but they're as different as, say, fiction and theater. And besides that we now have two ways of understanding poetry, through reading and through listening, I mean we always did but reading tended to blank out listening because it feeds in to the thinking part of the mind more easily and so maybe we stopped hearing poetry and maybe there's a kind of understanding through hearing that's different but as important. If you follow."

"I forrow. Prease erabolate."

"As a matter of fact." The subject was on his mind lately because of computers and CD-ROMS. "I was just thinking about this, because now I write with computers. What I was thinking was that computers are very visual. It's partly that it's very easy to incorporate graphics with text. But it's more that you become aware of text as a plastic entity, especially as you shift it around or change fonts, while with the solidity, inalterability, and regularity of the page as a block of print on paper the graphic element of the text, the fact that you're looking at it as well as understanding it, cancels out. Except for poetry of course. The hidden strength of modern poetry, hidden because it's so obvious, is that it's written for the eye, print designed on page. No matter how much we make a song and dance out of it, our tradition is written, not oral."

"Same with Asian ranguages!" she cried. "This is ow tladition of carriglaphy."

"That's right. But this just brings up the whole thing I was leading up to, the question of what is writing to begin with. The notion of calligraphy makes it explicit. Especially since now with computers we also can work with electrocalligraphic dimensions of writing. Electronics are refocusing us on the centrality of reading and writing. Instead of phoning now we e-mail or fax. Instead of watching TV we get on Internet. In a way it's irrelevant how much of it ends up as print on page. This is typically what happens when a new medium is introduced. The new medium doesn't wipe out the old, on the contrary, it just creates more options, and the older ones become more essentialized because they no longer need to be concerned with what the new mediums do better. Monet didn't stop painting with the advent of photography and take up the camera, he just became more painterly."

"Ah yes, in Japan we rike Monet vely much. Wataw rirries. We think is very suttor."

"What is suttor?"

"Suttor, is an Amelican wold. Meaning dericate shades of meaning. Nuance in Flench. In Japan we appleciate not being hit on head with what we see. This is a big plobrem with Amelican curtcha. You find this even in Larf Wardo Emelson. What herp flom thought, he asked. Rife is not diarectics."

"Yes, but he also said, I now seem to remember, People disparage knowing and the intellectual life, and urge doing. I am very content with knowing."

"But arso, Vely content with knowing, if I onry could know. So you know something about Larf Wardo Emelson." She looked at him in a different way.

"It's been a long time since I read him."

But now something very mysterious began to happen. They had in fact been stopped for a while in front of the Pyramid Club, maybe the driver was too discreet to break into their conversation. Waldo began to feel something familiar spread through his body. At first he didn't recognize what it was, maybe because it had been some time since he felt it. His whole body was being sensualized, as if it were one large sexual organ. He felt it first in his arms and legs, then it spread to his belly and groin. His lips and tongue became engorged, his sex started to throb. He had often been called a prick, now he was starting to feel like one. He knew she was doing it but he didn't know how she was doing it. In fact she wasn't doing anything, just sitting next to him hands in her lap. She wasn't looking at him, on the contrary her lids were lowered. And he didn't even think she was very pretty on first impression, there seemed to be something awkward and bow-legged about her, something almost clumsy, while her face did not fit his preconceptions about beauty.

"I would like to make a drawing of you," he said.

"Ah? You can dlaw?"

"I can write. And drawing is an extension of writing. Or can be."

"You went to alt schoor?"

"You don't need to go to art school to draw. No more than you need to go to penmanship school to write. You've heard of Art Brut?"

"Naturary. Outsida Alt."

"Sometimes also called Self Taught Art. In France they call it Art Brut. I think of the American version as Art Brute, like grafitti is a good example, and a good example of writing as a kind of drawing. A kind of calligraphy. The writing of the future will move from language to graphics and back again without any problems. It's already happening with Windows and Mac. The key is the idea that you can have writing without language."

"In Asia we have. And you have Ezla Pound and his ideoglams. and e.e. cummings liting or ova the page. In Rattin Amelica and Eulop Cement Poetly. In Flance Apporinaire. Beautifoor. And in Engrand Seventeen Centuly I think."

44

"But the kind of writing I'm thinking of will escape categories. Especially the category of the beautiful. Beauty is only truth after the fact. And truth can only be eccentric and specific, as specific as DNA. What I see in your face is the truth, not the truth in general but the truth of your particular dioxyribonucleic acid which, given its role in reproduction, is very sexy to be in contact with. Your face shows your genetic fingerprint, you as eccentrically you. The opposite would be a *Playboy* centerfold, sex in general engendered by air brush. Or an identity depending on this year's style. That's why I want to draw you. Or, rather, write you, write you as Willem de Kooning might, or Jackson Pollock, escaping language altogether, not just partly, like Pound or cummings, but expanding our whole concept of writing to include kinds of expression beyond the reach of language alone, and, more important, kinds of intelligence."

"I think you velly suttor. I fear what you say."

"What's to be afraid?"

"Fear. Like you touching me. Fear."

He was starting to understand why she turned him on so. It was maybe because, withholding noisier kinds of erotic attraction, she allowed him to feel other less evident but more powerful forces of magnetism. She was letting her DNA talk to his DNA. Like, you can only feel gravity once you relax and stop trying to resist it.

This became obvious once they went into the club to catch the reading. It was sponsored by a self-proclaimed avant-garde literary press called Nude Erections. The first reader declared herself a multisexual, took her clothes off while reading her first poem, and read the next while masturbating with one of her high heeled shoes. She had a neat body so Waldo was surprised to find the performance totally unsexy and besides it made it hard to concentrate on the poetry, which he could only pick up in a snatch here and a snatch there. But there was an absurd humor about the reading that demystified poetry readings in general, or maybe just high heeled shoes. It could be considered a form of Art Brute, it struck him, in that it called into question accepted criteria of what was supposed to be good and what bad. Art Brute gets you quickly beyond the acceptable.

Even so, Waldo didn't enjoy the performance as he might have some other night. It wasn't suttor. Tonight he was tuned in to the suttor. The suttor operated at a higher frequency than the sonic poetry of poetry slams, and maybe also at lower ones. Unless a slam poem pushed in the direction of ear poetry. Poetry for the ear could operate on frequencies of the suttor. The same was true of page poetry for different reasons. Page poetry was too tuned in to the frequency of language, and that was a frequency that was all too frequent in his life, all he had to do was turn on the radio or walk into a classroom. Page poetry was usually too dependent on the language of academedia because it depended so much on loudly explicit communication. It's as if you said to someone you were trying to seduce, Let's jump into the sack, thereby missing the intricate modulations of meaning that, as in chaos theory, may be more powerful in the long run than the sledgehammer of information or the sharp knife of syllogism. While maxing rational info academedia minimized sensuous info and generated too much noise. Page poetry that pushed in the direction of eye poetry was a different matter, eye poetry could quiet things down enough so that you could hear something. Page poetry could also push in the direction of ear poetry or even in the direction of pure writing, like John Ashbery or the Language Poets. And when Waldo said poetry he meant writing in general, which he theorized was currently escaping conventional categories and expanding its field of expression in many directions at once.

Mieko was looking a little confused as she listened to the reader masturbating with her shoe. "This is a sram?"

"This is the beginning of a sram. I mean a slam. Afterwards they decide who got the most applause and that's the winner."

"Al hull poems lear?" she asked after the reader finished, bowed to the applause, and threw her shoe into the audience. "And al they good?"

"Are her poems real," Waldo repeated. He was beginning to understand the peculiarities of her pronunciation. "I'd say they're real if she had an orgasm. The test of a real poem is whether it has a real effect. She looked like she had an orgasm so I would say they're real poems."

"Prease erabolate."

"Fake poems are useless. Like having a fake orgasm. They may look like real poems but they're imitation poems, they have form but no effect on anyone except possibly the author as a kind of masturbation. But that a poem is real doesn't necessarily mean it's good. A poem, any good art, is good on the same basis that any other intellectual pursuit is good. It illuminates our experience, extends the range of our thought, adds to our knowledge, aligns feeling with reality, amplifies our emotions, moves us to act, etcetera etcetera. Just like history or philosophy, but more inclusive."

Before long they decided to leave and she asked if she could give him a ride home. "Where are you staying?" he asked.

"Hotel P Yeah."

"The Pierre? I live right next door." He spontaneously decided taking the wrong way home would be a right move.

"Too bad I didn't study Amelican Ritalatcha with you. You have good opinions."

"My best opinion is of you. The rest was all made up on the spot."

"You don't bereave?"

"What's the difference? Tomorrow I'll have more opinions, maybe other ones, maybe better ones."

"Then why say them?"

"Just to get you into the sack." It had been on the tip of his tongue. He knew he shouldn't have said it, but he had this wild urge to say what was on his mind, whatever it was. Much to his surprise, though, her response was to invite him up to her room for a drink.

After they looted the minibar, she said she had a language question. "What means 'into the sack'?"

Instead of explaining, he demonstrated. It began as an exercise in the suttor, but ended as Art Brute because Art Brute takes over and calls everything into question finally, even the suttor, and answers questions, when it answers them, in the most basic language, the language of DNA.

When he got home that night the roaches were fast asleep, you could almost hear them snoring peacefully in their burrows.

Next morning on his way out for a bagel he met Slumski. Slumski after lunch was bad enough, but Slumski before breakfast was too much. For some strange reason he liked Slumski, Slumski was such a blatant pig that he never tried to disguise his basic pig nature. Among his other virtues he was a lecher and he didn't hesitate to let on to Waldo's girlfriend that she could always pay her rent with her body if she was short of money. In fact, he was sitting on the stoop reading a copy of *Pigboy*, the glossy, mass circulation porn magazine.

"You're an illegal tenant, you got rent control, and you still don't pay your rent, whatever little of it there is. What's the story?"

"I'm waiting for a check to come in."

"Oh yeah! From where?"

"The magazine you're reading."

"You don't read this magazine, you look at it."

As a matter of fact he had sent a story to *Pigboy*. Two years ago. He was still waiting for a response. But, anything to stall Slumski.

"They said my story would be in the next issue."

"Oh yeah?" Slumski was impressed. His brutish little eyes narrowed to crafty slits. "A story? That you made up? What do they pay for a story?"

"A few thou," said Waldo off hand.

"Boy, are you smart. A few thou. I didn't know you were that smart. For something you just made up like that. How do you do it?"

"You think. But you think with your ears, eyes, nose, and throat, you think with your skin, you think with your prick, and above all you think with forgotten parts of the brain that only animals, children, and artists know about."

"I don't get it."

"That's because it doesn't make any sense. But that's another discussion."

"So don't forget when you get that check."

"I'll pay you soon as it comes in."

"Okay. But you're still not off the hook on rent control, so don't get too smart. Once I get a judgment on that you're outa here."

But Waldo wasn't as worried about it as he was yesterday, by that time he might be rivving in the Wardolf Astolia. And if not, he'd make another story up, another story that would channel his experience, intervene in his reality, maybe one that would change his life.

Dick and Eddie

when everything fallS apart it's invariably a sign that at another level everything is Coming together in A New way—as a collecTive Human sEnSibility, this is probably the only optimism available to us—phenomena that seem disruptively random from one point of view may look like a different order from another—whiCh is why rAndomizaTion is a hopeful beginning, an opporTunity, in short, a chancE—in any case, the mind has a low toleRance for disorder—or to put it another way, healthy minds have a hearty appetite for disorder, which they consume at a rapid rate

For example, in the above passage, the embedded capitalizations make no sense, unless you happen to SCAN them as a separate sequence. THE SCATTER method, a Sufi technique, provides a way of discerning nonlinear and subliminal order which otherwise seems like disorder. "Scan the scatter," the subliminal message above.

In order to learn to see novel orders, it may become necessary to unlearn old orders. The sequence and placement of words on a page, e.g. Non sequitur is a valuable rhetorical figure in this sense because it is disruptive and forces one to look for novel order. The same is true of ellipsis. Life is often just a series of non sequiturs and ellipses that we bridge to get from one moment to the next. Minimalizing risk, the risk of the unfamiliar, the strange, the unknown. But suppose we didn't? We'd get from one moment to the next anyway, but some other way, maybe a better way. Some way maybe less glib. More dangerous. Leaps instead of bridges.

Landing in unexpected places.
This is
what stories are about, or should be.

Unpredictable.

But never ending up nowhere because wherever there is a where
there is a there. Too many stories end up where you know they'll end
up. He said. Walking over to the

windows
and
gazin
g
thoug
htful
ly at
the
citys
cape.
A
ferry
was
comin
g in
from
Hobok
en,
the
day
so
clear
he
could
see
its
flag
rigid
in
the

stiff
breez
e.

Eddie was not fascinated by his impromptu lecture. But knowing his need to be authoritative about everything, she was willing to indulge him with an attentive air, nodding gravely now and then, all the while wondering how soon, and how, he would get around to making love to her. She supposed he'd brought her up to his fiftieth floor apartment with its spectacular view of the New York skyline for ulterior motives. Or at least she hoped so. It had been fifteen years, and Eddie wasn't assuming anything. It was quite possible that his explosive sexuality had gone grey with his hair. She had once seen him suddenly start making love to a blonde in the middle of a party, the other guests quietly leaving the room one by one when they realized he wasn't going to stop. By the time the blonde realized he wasn't going to stop she was alone with him in the room and mostly undressed. The blonde hadn't been wearing much to begin with so the undressing didn't require a huge effort. But he was adroit and Eddie was fascinated, though not probably as fascinated as the blonde. Eddie felt she had the right to stay and watch since she was his date. It's true it was their last date, but that was for other reasons.

He droned on about order and disorder. Eddie didn't understand any of it. When he talked this way the words seemed to be in a book, then began to scatter on the page, the page itself began to shatter. That was why she'd stopped going out with him fifteen years ago, it was because he gave her the willies. It was practically hallucinatory. She began seeing their conversations instead of hearing them and then the words would dissolve, resolving into alphabets in the air, composed of changing fonts depending on his tone and emphasis. Now it was happening again, she had to wonder whether it was worth it, even for the sake of a terrific fuck, like one of their fucks of yesteryear. Eddie blamed herself for being oversexed and getting into pickles like this, while at the same time she had to admit that she liked being oversexed. A lot. Even after fifteen years she had this clear memory of his dick. Maybe that was because his name was Dick. Maybe what she was really remembering was his name. She was getting confused. That was the effect he'd always had on her. She suspected it was because he was confused himself.

51

I'm confused myself, he said, plucking the words, as it were, from her whirling mind. But, he continued, I prefer to be confused. You probably think I'm crazy.

I've always thought you were a little crazy.

You may be right. But I'd argue for a superior epistemological sanity and I'll tell you why. Because it's precisely those moments of deepest confusion that reveal breaks in an inadequate pattern of order, *aporia*, like the man says, allowing us to explode the cliches of narrative that lead us away from rather than into the data of our experience. And it's exactly those false narratives that drive us crazy by betraying our experience, often to the benefit of the powers that maintain the status quo.

Very intriguing, she ventured.

Take our story, just for an example, he went on. You may have an idea of what is supposed to happen next, I don't. Do we quote renew old bonds? Do we quote disappoint one another's expectations? Do we quote take up where we left off? Do we massage one another's nostalgias? Do we enter into a suicide pact, make passionate love and leap from the fiftieth floor? Or will it be something neither of us could have guessed the moment before?

Let's order in Chinese, she said. I'm hungry.

He slapped her lightly, almost playfully, on the cheek. Could you have foreseen that? he asked, standing over her. None of us know for sure what's going to happen next.

She responded by punching him the balls, mustering enough leverage from a sitting position so that he doubled over. For example, she said.

To the point, he groaned. Which do you prefer, Szechwan or Cantonese?

Cantonese, it's easier to spell. What was that bit about benefitting the status quo?

Let's be blunt. The rich and the powerful have a big stake in maintaining things as they are, or failing that, in making sure that any change is managed change, under their management of course. And that includes how you say, what you look, when you hear, even where you feel. It depends on timing. Try changing the look of words on a page twenty years ago and all hell breaks loose. I know, I tried. Try it today and nobody notices because narrative is an ongoing process, and one of the things that goes on is an ongoing process of incorporation. But it's a process like an eddy in a stream that can swirl back to recollect what's gone before and use it in a new cycle in a new way. Time reverses itself all the time, relativistically speaking. Narrative is never straightforward, except in America, or so we like to think. In America narrative drives straight ahead, perpetually on the interstate. Here everything we do is done for the first and last time, if you want to eddy back to the past try Europe. Here the attitude toward tradition is we've done that already, forget it. Everything we do is unprecedented, nothing has a lineage, we reject not only the mother and the father but the very idea of parentage. Fuck the past. The trouble is that makes us all orphans. You can't have a future without a past. That's why we're always on the interstate, which is an undefinable state between the past and the future. That's why it's both interesting and terrifying to be an American. It's like a speeding car with no brakes. The American narrative is not so much an eddy as a tornado, cutting loose with an erratic course across the landscape of time, the most dangerous force in the world. So everything I said before still goes only the stakes are higher.

Speaking of steaks, I'm hungry as a Hungarian, she said, and my appetite for talk is limited.

HALF-TIME INTERLUDE. WE WILL RESUME PLAY SHORTLY, AFTER THE FOLLOWING ANNOUNCEMENT.

And now, please stand. I would like everyone reading this, or hearing it, to please stand up and raise your right hand. Repeat after me: I fudge obeisance to the snag, of the unwritten snakes of the hemisphere, and to the onion from which it screams, one masturbation, invisible under snot, with liberty and justice for some. Please be seated.

AND NOW, BACK TO DICK AND EDDIE

They decided to go out for tabouli. He said it was a subliminal craving aroused by the scent of her perfume, which was called Taboo. He said taboos were made to be broken. He said he never let a day go by without breaking some taboo. On principle. Preferably as soon as he got up in the morning. If he let it get too late in the day sometimes he wouldn't get around to it, or at least not till late at night, and sometimes not at all.

Isn't that just a little compulsive? Eddie wondered.

Not compulsive, he replied. That's my job, the job of the, well, what am I exactly? A construction worker. The first step in construction is demolition. It comes hard to most people but actually it's quite easy once you get the hang of it. It looks complicated. The trick is to find the point of leverage. Then one tiny thrust, a little spurt of energy, an involuntary spasm, is enough to send the whole Oedipus tumbling down. Fuck the past. But don't expect any thanks for it. Even though the moment of destruction and the moment of recreation are one. That's why artists are problematic. Recreation for them means problems for us.

Is that it? asked Eddie.

No, that's just the beginning, responded Dick. That's just clearing the ground. Then you have to dig the hole.

The whole what?

That depends. Whatever you see as holistic. It can be a black hole or holy as a Swiss cheese.

I prefer it be wholesome.

Yes your holiness. You've always had a moralistic streak. The trouble with you moralists is that your efforts are misplaced. Why tell people what or what not to do when they don't know how they think? Moralists believe that thinking is something like arithmatic, right or wrong, get the logic right and it all adds up. Syllogisms. But let's examine that word. When you realize it's a compound of silly and gism its meaning breaks down. Am I going too far? Do you follow?

At a distance. A great distance.

What I'm talking about is just a different way of looking at things. The way most of us look at them most of the time. Not thinking about their meaning. Looking at them instead of through them. This is called the holy see. Why does it seem so crazy then?

They put on their coats and went down in the elevator. She could feel her ears pop as it descended. But instead of going to the restaurant he directed the taxi to the South Street Seaport. There were plenty of restaurants over there also so she didn't complain, but when she found herself at the end of a pier with him she did think to inquire. What the hell are we doing out here?

He didn't answer. There was a light fog over the East River but she could see a small tramp steamer, high in the water, plugging upstream against the current. The foghorns and buoys were hooting and piping in the Upper Bay. Humidity created an illusion of sweatiness on the slightly swaying wooden pilings, as if they were laboring. Just then a large launch pulled in and he ushered her down a long flight of wooden steps. A short man with a limp wearing a yellow plastic slicker helped them onto the boat's lightly rolling deck and into a sizeable cabin. The sailor at the wheel didn't turn around. All they could see of him between his stocking cap and the collar of his pea jacket was a massive neck, purplish and creased like an elephant's trunk. The launch cast off quickly and its prow tilted up as it headed full speed out into the middle of the dark river. Before long they drew abreast of the tramp steamer she'd seen from the pier. Close up her rusty hull looked a lot bigger. She was floating well above the water line, and even in the dim light they could see a good part of the rudder exposed beneath her stern. The name painted on her bow was CYCLONE. A ladder clattered down the scaly side of the hull and they scrambled up. Luckily Eddie was wearing her jeans and Reebok high tops and even with that she felt slightly terrified as she slipped and lurched with the motion of the ship. At the top a sailor grabbed her arm and pulled her on board, Dick close behind. They were shown to the bridge. The captain, peering into the murk beyond the bow and muttering orders to the sailor at the wheel, didn't deign to greet them.

Why are we here? demanded Eddie of no one in particular. The captain had a full white beard, short, like Hemingway's.

The interesting thing about the rivers around New York is that they're reversible, said the captain. With the tide. He had a deep voice, like Henry Kissinger's without the accent, sepulchral. Today is my birthday, he continued, his eyes drilling into the darkness ahead. On my birthday a year ago I was navigating down the Amazon. My ship had no radar, instrumentation was extremely rudimentary. Down there sailing is much like an art form. A feeling of rightness is critical, because things happen too quickly to compute. You have to act before you think, like playing tennis or basket ball. Navigating becomes a matter of intuition, of judgment, almost of style. Style is not a question of what you put in, it is based on leaving things out, in this case snags and shallows. Style precedes thought and creates the frame in which new thought can occur. What do you like for breakfast?

Breakfast, come on, said Eddie. I have an appointment on the Upper West Side early tomorrow morning.

Sorry, said the captain. You won't make it.

She turned to Dick. I don't get it, he said. I didn't know this was going to be overnight. I thought it was a trip around the island. It was supposed to be a lark. There must be some misunderstanding, he said to the captain. You can imagine how he felt. A large tug churned past well off their port bow. He thought of signalling but knew it was useless.

Of course, a misunderstanding, said the captain. There always is, that's normal. That's just one reason why the story is always beginning again, forking, heading off in new directions. What exactly is the beginning, middle, and end of a voyage on a tramp steamer such as this I ask you? The whole concept is nonsense. You unload at a port while taking on new cargo which is unloaded elsewhere. Every port is end, beginning, and middle depending on whether you are looking forward back or around. Or you might best say that we inhabit a permanent middle. Our course? Right now we are headed for Long Island Sound, then past Montauk and Block Island into the open ocean.

What are you telling me? screamed Eddie.

You find that disturbing? said the captain. Some might find it sexy.

I arranged this with my travel agent, said Dick, and you turn out to be some kind of pirate? Or what's the story?

That depends largely on the feedback. If you're missed, that's one thing. If nobody notices, that's another.

You're thinking ransom? asked Eddie. Forget it.

I'm thinking money, said the captain. I'm going to create a story for you that we can sell to Hollywood. That will justify everything. Give meaning to your life.

What meaning?

The meaning is money. The means is money. The message is money. A long time ago I shipped out under an old Norwegian captain. He idealized the Vikings. He had in his cabin a whole library devoted to the exploits of the Vikings. Rape and plunder. He said they would descend on the coastal towns like a whirlwind, destroying what they could not carry away. Those crazy boys, he would say, shaking his head. We were carrying a cargo susceptible to spoilage, dairy products as I remember, yet he detoured over a hundred miles to pick up the passengers and crew of a pleasure yacht in distress, in face of an oncoming hurricane that he knew might prevent him from retracing his course in a timely way. Without hesitation. Then we had engine trouble, went adrift, radio dead, near run out of food, and drinking water was in short supply. We were down to dog snacks, part of the cargo. Before you knew it we were at one another's throats. The two young women from the yacht were trading their bodies for dog food. After a while there were so little rations some of the men just took their bodies when they pleased. We were devolving into bestiality. The old captain tried to restore order but the sailors knocked him on the head and plundered his cabin. He was dead by the time we were picked up, but the received version was he fell on his head. Twenty-three days adrift. After it was all over one of the young women sold the story to a magazine for a nice sum, I'm told, then got a film option on top of that. Ended up doing endorsements for a dog food company, developed quite a nice bark. So how does it all add up? The captain heaved a sigh. When I began it was all people, he said. Now it's all corporations. So it's important to have a track record, and I can show that I know how to take a catastrophe and turn it into a money making proposition.

Do I understand that you're heading for disaster again? Dick asked quietly.

You get the drift, answered the captain. And that's why I need you two. For human interest.

FEEDBACK FED BACK

The Norwegian freighter episode, speaking of human interest, was actually a trip I took with my ex-wife, with whom I remained deeply if ambivalently attached. She died recently of breast cancer. She always used to complain that I didn't put her into my stories. So here she is, now that it's too late.

Other personal messages are embedded in the text. I believe our reality is now largely a corporate one, mediated by the profit drive of the free market in almost every aspect of our lives. Therefore even autobiography has become a commodity, as, to wit, the above.

The story about making love in the middle of a party is true. It happened after a reading I gave at the University of Iowa Fiction

Workshop. Maybe it was my way of saying fuck you to the Iowa Workshop, which I didn't like because of its complicity in the literary-industrial complex that manufactures prestige with the power of money. Anyway, it was a memorable fuck, if only because I remember it.

The old captain in fact liked to read about the rape and plunder perpetrated by his ancestors, but he didn't like rape and plunder itself. However it's arguable that in our era the difference between enquote real experience and mediated experience is disappearing. Thanks to the electronic revolution, our experience of the text (or screen) is as real as any other experience. The print world is separable from the mind, but as it becomes continuous with the world of electronic media, the electrosphere—i.e., our reality—the distinction between mediated and unmediated experience begins to blur.

A film was recently made about the true story of stranded travellers in the Andes resorting to cannibalism and the survivors became heros. In Colorado where I live the sole survivor of a snowbound nineteenth century travelling party, though not broadcasting his exploit, was not so lucky, being sentenced by a judge who reportedly told him, with some irritation, "There was only three Democrats in Gilpin County, and you, you son of a bitch, you et two of em."

I travelled on the Amazon last year on a passenger ship made from the salvaged nineteenth century hulk of a Scottish steamer powered by a rebuilt engine from a caterpiller tractor. It had no instrumentation at all and at night the captain navigated with the sole aid of a strong flashlight.

I didn't notice the echo between my heroine's name, Eddie, and that of Oedipus. Does this imply some complicated trans-sexual taboo violating ambivalence? Probably. I'll have to think about this.

> Suppose we start leaving things out, she
> Suppose we   he answered.
> Right here? she asked, as she   her blouse.
> Why   felt each   under a life boat.
> But the weather   before they   dawn

They were, as a matter of fact in   at   o'clock,
eastern standard   The sea was   clouds   horizon
     black.   The waves began to   balance. Soon
          greenish pallor   doubled over the railing
all day   When night closed   The captain
     The radio
          the life boat   sea   now boiling
     life preservers   captain   lowered
boats   whirlpool   going down
     your whole life passes

this is what it's like to move into the end game, was what was
going through his mind. She was like an eddy in time that cycled him
back fifteen years. He had said goodbye knowing it was a mistake, but
sometimes every available option is a mistake. He remembered she
cried quietly, not to make a thing of it, and he was surprised that her
feeling reflected his, which he had never declared, even really to himself.

> I literally bumped into her in a museum.
> We were both looking at a Monet paint-
> ing of water lillies, one of those paintings
> where the colors swirl about and you
> can't tell up from down or reality from
> reflection. But we recognized one another
> immediately, not that we could exactly
> place one another, but we knew one
> another, knew we had been lovers, knew
> that we had liked one another and
> instantly knew that we still liked one
> another. Over coffee we caught up on one
> another's lives but what was eerie and at
> the same time vastly reassuring was the
> intuition that at times time doesn't matter.
> Even though it does.

> None of this was pre-
> dictable. A chance meeting
> set off a chain of specula-
> tion and invented incident

that quickly took off in directions of its own. Because you can never step in the same river twice, even though you are part of the river. I don't understand any of this. I don't need to. My mission is transmission. This is merely data.

Before I end this I want to say
Tho' you've gained zilch from my work today
That this is a narrative informed by gnosis
Where most stories mainly induce hypnosis
So unless your reading jogs you awake
You know de facto the writing's fake
The truth of fiction is now corrupt
So let it rot while you
                    WAKE UP!

Narralogue on Everything

When Waldo looked up from one of the books he was reading—it was his habit to read several at once—to gaze out the glass wall of the apartment he was borrowing—which was on the thirty-sixth floor of a building in lower Manhattan facing Wall Street and the World Trade Center—the skyline told him a story. It was the story of Euroamerican culture told through its architecture. Through his windows he could see examples of every period from Classical Greek and before to Postmodern and after. He was tickled by the immediacy with which the cityscape resolved itself into narrative, by the way he could get so much more information out of things by regarding them as dynamic rather than static, unfolding through time. Maybe it was because of the article by Hayden White he'd just been reading: "To raise the question of the nature of narrative is to invite reflection on the very nature of culture and, possibly, even on the nature of humanity itself. So natural is the impulse to narrate, so inevitable is the form of narrative for any report of the way things really happened, that narrativity could appear problematical only in a culture in which it was absent—absent or, as in some domains of contemporary Western intellectual and artistic culture, programmatically refused."

Waldo put that together with a bit of Emerson he had just come across: "The student is to read . . . his own life as the text, and books the commentary"—as ongoing autobiographical story and interpretation; and that with another from a new book of criticism by Richard Walsh: "The argument, not the content, is the site of a fiction's aboutness"—the dynamic, not the static, comprises fiction's meaning.

And it suddenly struck Waldo that what he was on to, that where his train of thought was heading, was not merely toward the relative trivia of the fictive imagination and the way it functions, but toward a momentous shift in the nature of understanding itself. Or to put it another way, maybe the intelligence of the Twenty-first Century was ditching static abstraction for experiential dynamism.

Or to put it yet another way, maybe narrative thinking with its experiential matrix was a more august mode, with vastly more intellectual power, than he had previously thought.

What ever happened to "minimalist" fiction? with its retreat to the brass tacks of a mean realism? Waldo turned to his computer.

E-MAIL TO A YOUNG NOVELIST: While it's true, Waldo, as you note I have said elsewhere, that writers today are well-advised to undertake their own promotion and that rather than adding up to "selling out," this amounts to taking charge of one's own reputation instead of allowing it to be exploited by the marketplace—while this is true, it's also true that the marketplace is inimical to serious thought, even when it celebrates it, because the market proceeds by other parameters. So while Warhol & Co. liberated us from anxiety about achieving marketplace success, so prevalent in the Fifties and Sixties with their morbid fear of "co-optation," one shouldn't confuse it with artistic success. In fact we all now know that worldly success is a wonderful thing that puts us on a par with powerful executives, rich business men, politicians, celebrities, and winners of the lottery, so it may be time to refocus on more surprising things. Does this answer your question? Feel free to get back to me on this. Yours, Ron Sukenick.

Waldo returned to his reading. "Life is a series of surprises," Emerson wrote, "and would not be worth taking or keeping if it were not." Elsewhere: "growth comes by shocks." In his journals, according to his exponent, Lee Rust Brown, "revelation shares the page with routine details; quotations jostle alongside new insights; hard facts border on dreams of the night before. It is inevitable that significant patterns emerge."

But they don't emerge by sitting on your backside, metaphorically—and maybe even literally—speaking, thought Waldo. The surprise comes in the dynamic. "The quality of the imagination is to flow, and not to freeze," Emerson wrote in "The Poet," and the flow of imagination is our best vehicle for tracking the flood of experience, which abstract thought merely freezes and falsifies. Waldo was a fundamentalist of the book: he believed books should be literally true. The way people believed that the Bible was true. People believed that the Bible meant what it said, even if they didn't believe it. Belief was a choice, but the intention of the Bible was not metaphorical. To be sure its meaning could lend itself to metaphor, or allegory, or interpretation, or mystical flights, and no doubt should—but of these the ideal Book is innocent: it is not a metaphor, it is not a representation, it is not an illusion, it is not an imitation, it is what it is. In this respect a fiction is just like any other discourse—you would not say that an argument represents anything other than the argument, and so with fiction. The Word Is, simple as that. And here the current of Waldo's argument with himself was diverted to eddy for a moment around the difference between representation and reference, because stalwarts of the mimetic were always building their arguments for snapshooting experience on the seemingly solid ground that language can't help but represent—but Waldo found this sophistic, not that he had anything against sophism—to the contrary—because it was reference, of course, that language couldn't avoid—representation was quite another—mimetic—matter.

Above all, an argument is not static—a static meaning "soon becomes old and false," Emerson. And in fact, "all language is vehicular and transitive, and is good, as ferries and horses are, for conveyance, not as farms and houses are, for homestead." So Waldo was a proponent of narrative thinking, though he knew that the faculty he was after, as a basic manifestation of the imagination, needed a better name—argument? discourse? rhetoric?—as the term "imagination" needed thorough deconstruction. So, according to Emerson, it was in the nature of language to flow, and it was in the nature of meaning to flow, and that must mean that ideas are dams against that flow, attempts to husband, control and redirect it. But in fact we are finding that dams are less ecologically sound in the long run than we had thought. "'Every thought is also a prison,'" Sukenick quotes Emerson in his little-known book, *In Form*, marvelling at the Emersonian bravura, "because a thought, once formulated, becomes an impediment to thinking. . . . It is a matter of valuing the process of thinking over any particular idea, even a good idea. It is on this basis that the poets are—quoting Emerson again—'liberating gods,' why 'they are free and,' pun intended, 'make free,' why the poet 'unlocks our chains.'"

Sukenick was in India, communicating via the most efficient medium available in the circumstance, which is to say e-mail. Waldo was not sure why Sukenick was in India—all he had said on the subject was that it was less like any other place than he had ever been. But something in this stream of thought reminded him of an earlier e-letter from Sukenick. He went back to it on his computer.

E-MAIL TO A YOUNG NOVELIST: Mallarmé once observed that if a reader of average intelligence and no literary training read one of his books claiming to understand it, there would have to have been a mistake. Here in India the tradition is not that the writer write down to the audience but that the reader read up. If there is nothing for the reader to stretch the understanding, then what is there to learn? Not only is it taken for granted that literature provides a learning experience, it is also expected to be a healing experience, purging bad karma and leading to *moksha*, liberation. (Do we know the full extent to which Emerson was shaped by Indian thinking?) So literature is not isolated in the museum of art, surrounded by the ocean of entertainment—on the contrary, it's expected to shape personal and social values. I find this stance and all its implications sympathetic. Literature should not try to mirror our experience, it should intervene in it. It should help the reader understand himself and in so doing release the reader's repressed spiritual unconscious. In so doing the writer in the Indian view is conceived to serve as an example of virtue. The narrating poet in the *Bhagavad-Gita* is a role model, as opposed to the attitude in the *Republic* where the poet is regarded as the enemy of society. But this is consistent with a culture like India that sees itself as contemporaneous with its history and a participant in its narrative, immersed in its flow, rather than, as in the States, the end of its history, the culmination of it, from which perspective it feels free to disneyfy, ignore, or even annihilate it, as much as declaring that it no longer exists. The Indian attitude you can see written in its streets, where incarnate examples of every era from the Stone Age to the Postmodern seem to co-exist without any trouble. Yours, Ron Sukenick.

Waldo noticed that it was about time to take his enquote walk. There were two major things he liked about the apartment he was house-sitting for Sukenick. One was the fact that it was up so high he could get a wonderful disengaged overview of things, and the other was that it was next to the Hudson River along which he could walk aware of, and within, the flow of things. The only problem was he had trouble disentangling his own trains of thought from those of Sukenick, whose books he was surrounded by, whose atmosphere he breathed. One of the books he was reading was Sukenick's *In Form: Digressions on the Act of Fiction*, which he'd never seen before, and to what extent its drift was feeding the flow of his own stream of consciousness was hard to say. But the stream of his consciousness seemed to have a life of its own, and he was reluctant to rein it in. It was easy to let it loose up in the apartment on the thirty-sixth floor with its overview, where he felt abstracted from the risky contingencies of life in the city. But down there, next to the river, who knows where following your mind's nose could lead. Down there he was no longer in control, there were too many variables, it could get scary. Especially when he was trying to rein in the dogs. Usually he could handle them by letting them do what they wanted. That was his job, after all, letting them do what they wanted, mainly shit and piss. But sometimes they got a little rambunctious, or if they encountered other dogs, forget it, sometimes hell broke loose.

But Waldo liked adventure. He had known from an early age that he was more interested in excitement than stability. If he had been gifted with a talent for sports he probably would have been a whitewater type, surfing the rapids. He liked life in flood, undammed, unruly. He liked experience tuned up to an intensity that was on the edge of control, and over the edge. This carried over into his art—he liked to think of himself as a practitioner of what he called "extreme writing." Waldo believed—he knew—that you couldn't get anywhere new without ignoring the rules and letting go. There was no other way to break out of what everybody already knew. Anyway that's what gave him a kick, that feeling of being out of control, the scary freedom of it, knowing that being out of his own control he was also out of anyone's control. It was his experience that once through the control barrier some other kind of sense began to take over, once he'd left behind the slowpoke mind other faculties began to kick in, faculties too quick for what we normally think of as thought, more like the intelligence at work in sports, or music, or painting. In fact, for Waldo, writing as art was a lot closer to any of those three than it was to writing as essay, though the challenge immediately presented itself of applying that kind of intelligence to the essay as well. But, on the other hand, Waldo didn't like to think about essay as art. He didn't like to think about anything as art, including art, because he believed that what we call art was a put-down catchall for a spectrum of intelligence beyond the narrow attention purview of our culture. Rhetorically Waldo was on the side of the aporia, the sublime, the unexpected—anything that reached beyond preconceived meaning.

What flood of formless drool would this take on writing produce if it were widely accepted? you may ask. But Waldo was not interested in what was widely accepted. Those who were going to produce formless drool would produce it in whatever form they chose. Waldo was only interested in those acrobats who could swing with the riskiest precisions but with nothing in mind, jazz improvisors, abstract expressionists, pomo innovators, hackers, hip-poppers.

Formless drool. Right. It was time to do it. Otherwise they'd be shitting on his clients' persian carpets and there'd be hell to pay. As a certified member in bad standing of the surplus labor army known as the Ph.D. glut, Waldo had been forced to take a series of ignominious part-time jobs to supplement his income from occasional teaching gigs. He was suffering from what he called adjunctivitus, thanks partly to old coots like Sukenick who refused to retire and make room for a new generation. The latest of these jobs was dog walking. Busy people out earning their livings paid him to take care of their pets' toilet needs. It was a line of work in great demand, it seemed. All Waldo had to do was post his Petset® flyers and he was deluged with offers. It was good to feel socially useful now and then, part of the free market economy. Scooping up dog shit. It was the best of his improbable succession of self-inflicted employment. Got him out into the fresh air. It was even better than pushing dope in Washington Square Park. Or selling soda cans he picked out of public trash containers.

But what is this spiritual unconscious that Sukenick seems to insist on, that his stream of thought keeps eddying back to? Could it be related to Emerson's idea of focus as described in that laughably clumsy passage about becoming a "transparent eye-ball. I am nothing. I see all"? What an awkward and grandiose succession of strained, rupturing phrases. And yet. You can see what he's getting at. Starting with the notion of the "innocence of the eye," as Ruskin put it, enabling painters to see things "as a blind man would see them if suddenly gifted with sight"—that is, giving priority to the integrity of the senses—what Emerson is getting at is radical in terms of the way we think, proposing as it does a state beyond the normal level of consciousness that bypasses the individual ego and taps the extrapersonal, the universal. Why, it's practically shamanistic! If not Wordsworthian. "Mean egotism" vanishes and you become conscious of greater issues—Emerson calls them God—issues of crucial concern that most of the time for most of us lie dormant, and with which the serious writer with his eccentric concentration, her level of attention—his focus—puts us in contact. This must be what Sukenick means when he refers to "the holy see."

But there's another facet to Emerson's eyeball invocation: "I am nothing" when "I see all" is a strikingly passive formulation, reminiscent of Wordsworth's "wise passiveness," a phrase which, according to what Sukenick told him, Allen Ginsberg was fond of quoting with reference to the Beat point of view in distinguishing it from mainstream American aggressiveness. When you're passive you see things others don't because you're more receptive, attentive, there's less interference, especially from your own aggressive projections. In his book *Down and In: Life in the Underground*, Sukenick describes this aspect of the Beats and connects it back to Transcendentalism. *Down and In*, which Waldo found in Sukenick's apartment, is presumably a collective autobiography of the underground culture from the forties through the eighties—some say it's the definitive book on the era—but Sukenick told him he considers it a docunovel, a long, ongoing argument, and one of his best narratives, in fact an excellent model for narrative as argument. In any case, it's here, in this stance of receptiveness, "transparence," that Sukenick must base his taste for the random, the accidental, the fortuitous, trusting it to move him beyond the stale, the static, the status quo version into a fresh view of experience. And this without a qualm about inviting chaos— in fact he seems to entertain chaos as an opportunity to create new kinds of order since, as he wrote somewhere, the healthy mind has a prodigious appetite for disorder, which it consumes and metabolizes at a rapid rate.

Because disorder is just another word for experience—a crucial term for Emerson, and one which Sukenick is careful to substitute for reality on any occasion it's important to make the distinction—and experience is "the text of life"—a phrase Sukenick could have gotten from Wallace Stevens, who could have gotten it from Emerson. (Sukenick, he knew, had written the first major explication on Stevens, enlightening a generation of formerly baffled grad students, along with their profs. Waldo hadn't read it, he was happy with Helen Vendler's way of reading the poems backwards.) Experience is the text of life which the writer reads and transcribes ("life the text, books the commentary")—when his eyeball is transparent enough, that is. And as soon as you say experience you must say biography, or more precisely, autobiography, since it's only the self that can experience experience. So that the most original writing, the writing that gets closest to the river of experience, the way things happen, can only have an autobiographical base, a base, however, that "mean egotism" would deny by its petty impositions of meaning. And using experience as a base for knowledge can only lead in one direction, and that is toward democracy, while preconceived notions of reality, such as that implicit in imitation theories because they are hierarchic (reality is merely imitated by art,) and imposed, tend to the authoritarian.

Pleased to have gotten that settled, Waldo threw on his coat and was walking out the door when the phone rang. He ran back in and picked up the receiver. It was Sukenick, calling from New Delhi.

"What a coincidence," said Waldo. "I was just thinking about you and Emerson."

"Emerson is a bore," said Sukenick. "If you're going to sit around my beautiful apartment thinking about Emerson, instead of using it to get laid, you might as well be living in your shit hole on Loisida fighting the roaches. I'm at the airport. I'm coming back to New York. Next flight, in five minutes, with a stopover in London. Don't leave any dishes in the sink." Sukenick hung up.

Waldo was vexed. Not only was Sukenick giving him short notice, but in putting down Emerson he was demonstrating an obnoxious ignorance about his own roots. Take the sentence Waldo had just been reading from Emerson's ingenious exponent, Rust Brown: "Unafraid of contradictions, encompassing both critical commentary and experimental stances, Emerson's essays pursue biography equally by reporting on it and by provoking readers aggressively to further perceptions." What could be more sukenickian than that? Waldo was hurt. Like Emerson's writing, Sukenick's both reported on and created experience at the same time, why couldn't Sukenick see it. Waldo had to ascribe this blindness to Sukenick's streak of redneck anti-intellectual tendencies which were liable to break out at any time.

Redneck tendencies, Waldo mentally grumbled while locking the door and heading for the elevator, that seemed to stem from Sukenick's yahoo ideas about art and social wellbeing, his corny conviction that art in the long run could only justify itself by helping to create a culture that abetted the richness of common experience and encouraged social justice. Sukenick was not so stupid as to claim that art actually had this effect on the culture, only that it should try to have such an effect, even if it failed miserably to do so both in the short run and the long run. But from this conviction, Waldo was convinced, stemmed Sukenick's railing, for example, against the elitism and hermeticism of French criticism, even though Waldo knew for a fact that he liked a lot of French criticism and knew more about it than he let on. Waldo suspected that what he liked he liked because he saw in certain critics a prosier confirmation of certain directions he had taken much earlier than said criticism in his own creative work. Yet, yet, thought Waldo as he savagely poked the elevator button, yet he had the chutzpah to bitch about such august philosophes as Philippe Sollers, leader of the eminent Tel Quel group, as an amoral opportunist. Granted that Sukenick spent much of his time in Paris and might know something that he, Waldo, didn't know, but Waldo felt Sukenick's vituperations on this score came out of his somewhat primitive ideas about esthetics and democracy. He knew that Sukenick's references to "the holy see" came directly out of the idea, if you could call it that, that art, by nourishing an inner life—archaic phrase—of self-awareness, reflection, and moral thoughtfulness, should awaken consciousness and therefore conscience, as opposed to entertainment, which narcoticized both. Maybe that was the source of attraction for Sukenick of art as argument, if not polemic, if not harangue.

But in all fairness, Waldo conceded as the door to the elevator slid open, he knew from the nasty critique of Thomas Mann's *Doctor Faustus* that Sukenick had let loose just before he left for India, that this was a vulgarization of his argument about argument. Because insofar as Waldo could remember Sukenick's argument about the Mann novel, his complaint was that it was on one side a blatant attempt to conform history to prefabricated doctrine, and on the other a denial, a disguise of that same doctrine by fobbing it off as a representation of experience. The argument was at the same time made and represented as something else, the nasty pill made palatable by its sugar coating. The result was—Sukenick's word—"phony." As opposed to some of Mann's earlier work, *Death in Venice* or *The Magic Mountain*, which are more persuasive as processes of discovery in which the argument is the evolving experience.

And here, as Waldo recalled, Sukenick expressed a peeve with a book he approved of, the recent *Novel Arguments* by Richard Walsh, about which he'd heard Sukenick mutter "They're finally beginning to get it right." What he remembered Sukenick saying was that Walsh's take on fiction as argument was still schizophrenic because he defined argument in fiction as interchangeably either form or content, a distinction Walsh in the same breath, as it were, argues against. It was a way, Sukenick claimed, of narrowing the import of Walsh's insight to a critical quibble when it impacted, as Hayden White observed, on the nature of culture and even of humanity, if we take thinking as the genius of the genus. Sukenick, on the other hand, I suppose, Waldo thought, would have given a much broader definition more in the tradition of rhetoric, a supposition he could support by quoting a book by Richard A. Lanham called *The Electronic Word*, which he found on Sukenick's active shelf with a piece of torn newspaper marking page 227, and the following underlined: "We have in the West a venerable tradition of studying how human attention is created and allocated: the 'art of persuasion' which the Greeks called rhetoric. . . . Whenever we 'persuade' someone, we do so by getting that person to 'look at things from our point of view,' share our attention-structure." I suppose such an attention-structure could be a story or a novel as well as a speech, thought Waldo. And for that matter, maybe narrative could usefully be regarded as exploratory oratory—the rhetoric of evolving experience. This thought put into perspective a remark Sukenick made about Walsh: "He says that the descriptive arguments placed at the head of old narratives were something like abstracts—I remember them as more like plot summaries." In other words, the argument is the action, according to Sukenick? Which may contain sub-arguments in a variety of forms, more and less discursive? Well, it's always hard to figure out exactly what Sukenick is talking about. Waldo's attention structure, as a recent graduate student, was focused on more cohesive writers than Sukenick who had undertaken the subject, undertakers like Paul De Man, Stanley Fish, Northrop Frye, I. A. Richards, Wayne Booth, and Kenneth Burke. He'd never had trouble understanding those guys—except maybe Kenneth Burke—so why should he have a problem with Sukenick?

What did come across though, in Sukenick's comments about Walsh, was Walsh's "generous"—Sukenick's word—quotation of Sukenick on "innovative fiction"—a term Sukenick seemed to take credit for putting into circulation, replacing the inaccurate and implicitly denigrating "experimental." The kind of fictive language Sukenick purveys, Walsh quotes him as having written, "simultaneously proposes and cancels itself, not to deny the autonomous reality of the world, but to salvage it from the formulations of language. The provisional nature of fictive language allows it both its imaginative freedom and its claim to truth. . . . affirmation of the medium has provided an authority for the way out of a modernist hermeticism back into an investigation of common experience." This is a key point, Sukenick claimed, in discussing fictive truth, a discussion normally conducted with profound superficiality. Narrative fiction makes contingent statements about the world—the only kind you can importantly make, when all is said and done—whose main virtue is that they displace even more contingent, less reliable statements while at the same time recognizing their own contingency. The model is rhetoric: a series of persuasive statements that displace less persuasive statements. Even the most blatantly fictive narrative—say, fairy tale—argues a situational veracity, I mean we are not necessarily talking about truth to fact. So, Waldo reflected, if I understand Sukenick correctly, the moment of truth in fiction is the moment of composition—or, as Sukenick would more likely put it, and does in his new novel, *Mosaic Man*, the hand writing on wall.

If this stance summons up an image of a runner running fast so he doesn't fall into the void, Waldo imagined Sukenick would answer that narrative is a dynamic form that sometimes runs fast, sometimes plods, and sometimes moves with deliberation, but must always be moving.

Anyone sharing Waldo's attention-structure, however, would now have to shift focus to his anxieties about dog walking and especially his apprehensions regarding Lord. Lord was the Saint Bernard he usually picked up first, and it wasn't that Waldo was worried about being bitten, rather he was afraid of being licked. Waldo was dog-droolophobic, and Lord had the biggest, wettest tongue he'd ever encountered in a dog. Lord had a habit of tongue painting Waldo with a gooey coat of warm slobber. If he could avoid being wetted down by Lord his next trial was to avoid getting his ankle nipped by Louella, the toy poodle who was an avid ankle nipper. Manny, Annie, and Fanny, the three Basset Hounds, were no particular problem except they were stubborn, especially about Swifty the Greyhound's tendency to sprint down the promenade along the Hudson River. By the time Waldo picked up this menagerie from their various apartments and got them down the elevator they were usually growling and yapping at one another and at him. Waldo's defense against this incipient chaos was to think about something else, anything else. The main idea was just to think, to create another attention-structure. As a novice novelist, Waldo had already discovered that the best way to create a powerful attention-structure was not to methodically construct linear arguments but to spin a web of interconnecting associations that creates what he referred to as a magnetic ambiance, pulling you in to a particular way of seeing things. This he knew, was what Sukenick called narrative thinking. Its practice included such complex rhetorical considerations as style, tone, and pacing. These could be considered—Waldo emitted a nasty chuckle over how much Sukenick would hate the phrase—attention management techniques. As much as could chiasmus, enthymeme, litotes, brevitas, petitio principii, post hoc ergo propter hoc, reductio ad absurdum, sorites, zuegma, or the arguments ad baculum, ad ignorantium, ad populum, and ad vercundium.

Sukenick, in Waldo's opinion, had a stubborn prejudice against methodical argument, saying that such argument of necessity left too much out, thereby leading to false conclusions. The best narrative, he said, despite the centripetal red herring of plot, is ex-centric—which might explain why the best writers are eccentric. Besides which, Sukenick would probably argue—and here Waldo agreed with him—method often won the argument and lost the audience. The point is you're not trying to make a point, you're trying to get people to think a certain way.

Waldo was now down the elevator and outside the building. The dogs were barking and snarling at one another and running every which way, heading for the hydrants and lamp posts. Waldo had to break into a trot to keep up with them. He figured he looked like the careening dog sled from hell coming down the street. But aside from trying to keep his balance as his arms were jerked this way and that, no problem, Waldo was thinking of other things. He was thinking about how he'd spent seven years getting a Ph.D. that loaded his mind with special knowledge, interesting in itself, but useless outside the closed system it was meant to address. I mean, what did it have to do with the price of dog food? Waldo wondered. Because he was now outside the closed system, with little chance of ever getting back into it. For which he could thank Sukenick.

His yapping, woofing, skittering, zigagging dog circus was now on the promenade along the river where the real action began. It was doodoo time. They seemed to favor shitting in the middle of the promenade, to the undoubted surprise and delight of unwary pedestrians. However, this was highly illegal and subject to big fines, a risky business since the promenade was well patrolled. But Waldo had a system. He'd bring along a supply of baggies, insert his hand in one, grasp the steaming turd and turn the baggie inside out around it. He'd then put it in his jacket pocket and deposit it in one of the waste cans placed at frequent intervals along the promenade.

It was Sukenick's fault simply because one day he'd come across one of Sukenick's books in a used book store, a collection called *The Death of the Novel and Other Stories*, and as he read it he began to change his way of looking at things. The message was in the title, really, signifying as it did that an argument was just another kind of story. And as Waldo read through the book and saw what Sukenick did with story, morphing it into pure argument at times, at times modulating back to story telling in various combinations with argument, but all contained within a narrative flow that was itself an ongoing argument—seeing all this in Sukenick's book, it finally hit him that there was, since narrative contained all these possibilities within its own potential, absolutely no need for a partitioned, self-contained practice of criticism or critical theory. And indeed, this thought had its correspondence in certain critical theorists Waldo admired, particularly Derrida, some of whose work in form approached narrative—*Glas*, for instance. This experience came as a blow for Waldo, who had just put a huge amount of work into finishing his dissertation—on *The Society of the Spectacle*—and even though he still would endorse his critical approach, he was simply tired of all that. If anything, his work on Debord, with its attack on the way the make-believe of spectacle tended to displace the reality it represented, prepared him for Sukenick's take on fiction. On top of which he suddenly realized that the reason he'd had so much trouble with his dissertation was that it kept wanting to turn itself into a novel—the novel he was now trying to write. So that even if there were academic jobs out there—which there weren't, or not many—he'd now have to apply for work to Creative Writing programs, for which he had absolutely no visible qualifications and, incidentally, little respect.

As usual, Louella, the Toy Poodle, was the first to hunch her back and do her doo. Waldo hunched over himself and put the baggie on the duty, scooped it up and stuffed it carefully into his pocket. Then it was Swifty, and ditto, but bigger. However, to Waldo's surprise the waste can that was usually on this stretch wasn't there today, so he'd have to wait till he hit the one next block to unload his pockets.

The other thing that impressed Waldo about *The Death of the Novel and Other Stories* was its use of the page as a graphic space to demonstrate the visual element of writing in various ways. This was in a book published in 1969, when tampering with the look of the page was a taboo that aroused all sorts of furies, as if the book were diddling with Gutenberg himself and the epistemology implied by the authority of print. Now, with the resources of the computer, Waldo was extending the graphics factor in the novel he was working on. In fact—and he was well aware of the irony—just as his dissertation had almost turned itself into a novel, the novel he was working on threatened to turn into a picture—or at least, a series of pictures. Waldo understood the situation but he couldn't do anything about it: he was constantly unloading the shit he'd accumulated in one discipline into the non-discipline of a new practice. And as soon as that practice began to develop rules and procedures for him he would move into still another new practice. God knows where it would all end up, wondered Waldo—sky writing? And what was the point? The point, as near as he could guess, was to move progressively into virgin territory where there were no rules, where a practice was not yet a discipline. There must be an easier way, thought Waldo. Yes, there is Waldo, and it's called improvisation, but Waldo didn't realize that yet.

Improvisation forces a relaxation if not elimination of rules, thereby inhibiting methodical thought and releasing what we sloppily call intuition—shorthand for another kind of thinking which, as Wallace Stevens once defined imagination, may best be thought of as "the sum of our faculties." Disciplines are very useful for closed systems—logic, philosophy, chess—but intuition does better with open systems, the kind of thing you come across in the study of chaos, complexity, fractals. And life is an open system. So is language.

The beauty of intuition is anybody can do it. It doesn't take a lot of institutional or specialized training (though it can be trained), and so it does away with the need for elites as well as avant-gardes and democratizes intelligence itself. Anybody can do it and, in fact, everybody does it. This democratization of intelligence was in line with the democratization of technique which, as Sukenick points out in *Down and In*, had a lot to do with the culture rebellion of the Sixties. But in order for intuition to work, reflected Waldo, you had to let in the random, and that was just what Waldo couldn't do and Sukenick could do so well—allow the random in and pick up on what Sukenick called "meaningful coincidence," that led the stream of thought to the unforeseen and unforeseeable, and validated what we call art as a form of intellectual discovery.

The net effect of all this, Waldo knew, is ultimately political, in that it sanctions forms of thought available to everyone, as opposed to making thinking itself the property of a class educated in a certain way. A way, to be specific, that can be traced to the Plato-Aristotle axis that confines the search for truth to the exercise of syllogism in the service of a single static version of experience. It has been said that this mode of thought was at least partly engendered by the spread of writing literacy in Greek civilization, but whatever, it is clear that the so-called arts proceed by other modes of intelligence that tend to threaten the primacy of written language as our official, as it were, arbiter of truth. But, on the contrary, is it not possible to extend writing into other domains of intelligence? And is not narrative thinking a way of doing exactly that? Waldo could easily contemplate such a practice—the problem was he couldn't execute it.

There was no waste can on the next block. And Fannie and Annie were already doing their thing. He had no choice but to baggie the two identical turds and stuff them into his anorak pockets on top of the others.

If Sukenick came down on the speech-acts side of the ancient debate between the philosophers and the rhetoricians—and the side he took was quite clear from the Laurencesternean subtitle of *In Form*: "Digressions on the act of fiction"—it was probably because for a practicing narrateer writing is inevitably an activity, both within and without the text. So whatever expertise Sukenick had on the subject of fiction came from practice rather than theory. But, reflected Waldo, most theory is theory of criticism, i.e., of reading, while the only theory that interested him now, as a budding novelist, was theory of composition, i.e., of writing.

Now Manny the Basset Hound was doing his thing, and still no waste can in sight. Nothing to do but bag the shit and stuff it into his already shit filled pocket, squishing it down so it would fit. As he did he noticed another walker, a woman, a block away on the almost deserted promenade leading a single dog on a leash. At least he thought it was a dog at first, a small dog, but as she came closer he realized it was not a small dog but a cat, a big, black, furry cat. And the woman was a very attractive woman, blonde, long legs showing under the shortest of miniskirts, white, pleated all around and, oddly in this chilly weather, bare legs, skimpy sandals, no coat or sweater— just a thin white silk blouse under which it was obvious she had no restraining lingerie. She carried a musette bag over one shoulder and as she drew close he could see that she had an abstracted expression on her face, as if she were musing about something, something that amused her. She had an olivey foreign looking face, maybe Italian, maybe Greek, and a soft glow seemed to emanate from her protruding nipples shedding an unearthly incandescence on Waldo. Strangely, the cat, a long-haired bushy tailed fellow, seemed to have no fear of the unruly and yapping dogs—on the contrary, when it mewed at them mildly they shut up and seemed to make way as it advanced.

Waldo said hello.

Her expression went from musing amusement to bemused, if musical, laughter. "Are those the hounds of hell, or what?"

Waldo couldn't tell how old she was, eighteen or thirty-eight, forty-eight, fifty-eight, but he found her insanely sexy. "Aren't you cold?" he asked.

"Yes I am cold. Would you like to warm me up?" Her cat rubbed against his leg, mewing.

"How would you like me to do that?"

"Use your imagination. You could recite some poetry, for instance." She had an indefinable foreign accent, very slight, that gave her voice a soft, musical lilt.

"Where are you from?"

"Heaven," she smiled, amused at her joke. Waldo noticed faint music in the air, probably from one of the party boats that plied the river, he didn't know how to describe it—an instrumental rendition of a muezzin's call almost lost in the distance.

"I'm a writer," he said for no reason he was aware of.

"I could tell that from a mile away. Do you want to write me something?" she asked in a sweet, irresistible voice.

"Here? I have no pen, no paper."

"Write it in the air with your voice. Write it on the river and let it disappear. Write it on my skin with your fingers."

Without calculation, without forethought, without hesitation, with the conviction of total rightness and a sure touch, he stepped up to her and put his hand softly on her bare thigh, letting it sink upwards as he heard her breath deepen, the cat mewing and rubbing against his leg as she slowly embraced him. When suddenly he remembered all the shit he was carrying around, fearful that it was all going to squish out of his pockets as her embrace tightened.

She felt the change immediately, rudely pushed him away. "What are you, some kind of rapist," she said in a raucous voice. "You meet a woman in the street and you try to feel her up? I should call a cop on you. I got my rape whistle with me." Her cat yowled.

"No, wait a minute, please. I was just kidding."

"I am not amused, sonny boy. I work in a museum and I see a lot of perverts like you. They seem to be turned on by dead art, I mean, I guess if you sit around all day copying old masters you get very frustrated and horny. So run along, Buster, I'll let you off easy this time."

She walked off down the promenade, wiggling her cute little ass at him, her cat waving its tail. The muse was not amused. Just at that moment Lord, the Saint Bernard, decided to take a crap and hunching his back, dropped one of his super-huge turds as Waldo, constipated with frustration, immobile as a statue, watched. Lord, proud of himself, pranced over to Waldo and began giving him a thorough drool job, coating him with a slimy layer of dog mucous.

He kicked Lord aside and all at once dropped the leashes he'd been holding on to tightly so that the yipping, straining mutts couldn't get away. Feeling the loss of tension, the dogs looked back at him. Swifty the Greyhound was the first to get the idea, giving a yelp of enthusiasm and galloping off into the distance. The others quickly caught on and scattered every which way to a dubious freedom, as Waldo turned and walked back down the river to his own, tossing bags of shit over his shoulder as he went.

Back upstairs in Sukenick's apartment, Waldo took the draft of the novel manuscript he was working on and threw it down the incinerator. Then he sat down at his computer and wrote the first line of a new version:

◆

Five years later Waldo was a famous novelist and Sukenick was considered by the purveyors of an entertainment nation, many with an attention span probably too short for genital intercourse much less for reading his books, an author of the kind of literary fiction nobody was much interested in any more. They seemed unaware of Sukenick's war on the literary that prepared the way for the current cash crop of hip-pop fictioneers. But nobody with the slightest insight into the bottom line considerations of the entertainment industry would accuse the latest generation of businessmen that ran it of having read anything so long as a book. However, these book-mongers knew very well what kind of fiction they didn't like—anything in print that didn't come up to the going standard of fictitiousness in the industry. Fictition is fiction as prevarication, imitation, fake, that is, lying. You either wrote fiction or you were "academic." Fictition meant blockbuster potential, possible movie deals, paperback deals, subsidiary rights deals, deals, deals, deals. Academic was code for small sales, that is under twenty thousand copies hardcover—which seemed big to Sukenick—no chain store distribution, no subsidiary rights, no movies, too hard to translate, no deals. Let's be frank, academic, like experimental, like literary, was a quality distinction, and the quality was money.

What else is new? But there is something new here, and Sukenick, a book publisher and review editor, knew what it was. While in previous periods you had to struggle to get good work through the commercial publishing apparatus, now, with the takeover of the industry by international infotainment conglomerates, you had to fight to maintain some vestige of independence for the apparatus itself—if for nothing else, then just to preserve the country's intellectual discourse and free flow of ideas. The infotainment industry preferred images to words, presumably because an image is worth a thousand words (and how many is a sound bite worth?) But one true word can undercut a thousand phony images projected as simulacra or spectacle. You would expect that writers, intellectuals, and academics would rise up as one and shout that word, but they don't. Maybe they're too dependent on the publishing apparatus to complain about it.

Does this mean no good books get published? With forty-five thousand books a year spewed out by the trade publishers, a few inevitably slip through, including now and then one by Sukenick. The question to ask, Sukenick knew, was how many didn't.

Waldo's books were among those that had slipped through. Waldo was doing well. Sukenick assumed he was doing well, though he hadn't seen him in several years. Every once in a while Waldo would call him up to say they had to get together, but not this week, he'd call back. Then he wouldn't call back. It was a routine. Sukenick had come to expect it. Every now and then Waldo would call to say he'd call back. But Waldo had a great sense of humor, it was one of the things that sold his books. The last time Sukenick saw Waldo Waldo told him he owed everything to Sukenick, that he couldn't have done it without him. Maybe that was why he didn't call back. Because for example Sukenick would find his own sentences in Waldo's work, only with different words in them, not to mention familiar tonalities and organizing ideas. But that was all right, in the arts ideas are cheap. That's because they leave too much out. When you're working with ideas if you don't understand something, by definition you leave it out. In the arts when you don't understand something that's what you're looking for. If you don't understand it put it in. That's the material you work with. What's the point of trying to understand something you already understand? The grope of art extends beyond its grasp. If you're really lucky you come to grips with something nobody understands, but that's a domain reserved for major artists. Usually you're just struggling with your own ignorance, and the work is a valuable record of the working intelligence as it bridges the gap between what you know and don't know. But a major figure, a Kafka, for example, makes a connection between the known and the unknown. Such a figure knows the value of the unknown and even the unknowable, and manages to contain much of it in the work, enabling us to get, as they say, the mind around it, to bring it to consciousness. To such a figure the unknown is a friend, a risky friend, a terrifying and exhilarating friend who does not answer invitations from ideologues.

So it was fine for Waldo to use Sukenick's methods. That was the way it was supposed to work, Sukenick knew. You take some predecessor's ways of working the material, and maybe the material itself, and you work it your own way—Sukenick had done it himself. Then you revile and denigrate that predecessor as much as possible to establish your own originality. You may go so far as to say the predecessor had stolen your ideas, although this gets tricky, but not impossible, if he died before you were born. American artists are especially good at this historical juggle since we're raised to feel that America represents the end of history anyway. Though Sukenick sometimes wondered if it would be better to have a supportive and nourishing rather than destructively oedipal relation with one's art ancestors.

Whatever the relation though, between influencer and influencee, there is always something that marks the original. It isn't pretty. The original always bears a scar, the scar of birth, the navel, testimony to emergence, possibly in struggle possibly in inspiration, but always in some kind of emergency. In the influencee this mark is always slicked down, prettied up, handled more adroitly and so easier to swallow. Because thanks to the original you know how to do it. The poor bastard who did it first didn't know how to do it and had to blunder and fumble to a certain extent to get it done. In absorbing the original you have to in some sense share in the birth process itself, which is not nearly so pleasant, but may be more instructive.

But what are we talking about here? Not literary criticism and not theory, which are specialized disciplines. We're talking about rhetoric, and there is no area of intelligent life to which it does not apply—which is why until fairly recently in the march of centuries it was the central discipline for all pursuits of knowledge. Today all disciplines still have their appropriate rhetorics, though not so labelled, even the sciences. The famous scandal about Velikovski's *Worlds in Collision*, discredited by the entire scientific community even though years later he turned out to be right about catastrophe and cosmic evolution, was clearly a case of his using the wrong rhetoric, you can tell that just from the title of his book.

Moreover we are not talking about the study of rhetoric but its use, that is, we're talking about composition. First of all, in rhetoric—and this carries over to "creative" writing—there are no rules, there are only rules of thumb. That's because—taking oratory as the key example—when communicating with an audience, everything is situational. You can't teach anybody how to make a speech, you can only teach him to respond to a variety of audience situations. You never know what's going to happen, you never know for sure ahead of time what's going to be appropriate, though often you can make some good guesses. "Creative" writing is also a situation. It's situated in the interaction among the writer, his mode of composition (handwriting, computer, or etc., each creates a different situation), his calculating mind, his spontaneous inventions, his feelings, his memories, his particular experience, social conditions, the historical moment, his sex, his state of digestion—you can get as complicated as you like here—and his imagined reader, if any—in other words, it's situated in the act of writing itself. The creative part is the way the writer allows all this to come together at the moment of composition. Anyone who comes to the writing situation with too many preconceptions that don't go out the window at the crucial moment is going to produce writing that's buried before it's dead. It's like, what do you do if you've prepared a funny speech and discover you're at a funeral? In this sense "creative" writing is always improvisation—that's what makes it creative. The difference between this kind of writing and so-called noncreative writing is that in the former thinking is simultaneous with the moment of composition while the latter is largely a report of thinking that's already been done. Thinking in the moment of composition calls up faculties distinct from those that dominate more logical thought. Less linear, more embedded in the situational flow, more experiential in that it involves enactment of situations, more open to the wisdom of the feelings and emotions, more dependent on the power of example, more open to preconceptual information registered by the senses, more responsive to the moment and what is said to be a form of very short term memory that defines the purview of the present, more governed by quick reflex and instinct, these faculties add up to the word intuition or maybe, imagination, and constitute a powerful alternative to abstract thought. It's not much of a stretch to see that they also form a base for narrative thinking.

In our time it was the Beats who first rediscovered this elemental literary factor. Their slogans for it were "first thought, best thought," and "spontaneous prose," their prescription to achieve it, fast writing and reintroduction of the bardic spoken word. Speech and fast writing as elements in composition were ways of preventing preconception from taking over, but they aren't the point, it's avoiding preconception that's the point and there are as many ways of doing this as there are good writers. But in their practice the Beat writers introduced a way of thinking that was increasingly absent from an intellectual situation dessicated and literary in the worst sense—and people responded to it in great numbers, basically because they recognized it's the way they think themselves, i.e., situationally and without much abstract claptrap.

Let me tell you a story about Sukenick. He was sitting at his desk staring at his computer screen, when for no good reason he remembered a line he'd written more than twenty years ago. Maybe he'd seen it somewhere recently, but he couldn't recall opening the book it came from in years. Yet the line was very distinct in his mind:

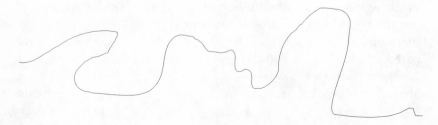

Where had he seen it lately?

Sukenick recalled what he had in his mind when he wrote the line. He'd had a bad case of semantic claustrophobia. He felt that language could no longer express what he meant. To make things worse, he didn't know what he meant. But the situation was vaguely familiar. He associated back to the tiny incident that he was persuaded turned him from a literary hack into a real writer. He was trying to write his first novel with not much success when, one day, he wrote something, he didn't remember what, then literally heard a voice in his head saying, *"You can't write that."* So he went back and crossed it out and completely forgot about it and forgot about the voice, as if nothing ever happened. The same thing, he figured later, must have happened many times before. But this time for some reason, maybe because he'd been reading Rabelais and Henry Miller and Laurence Sterne, two minutes later he remembered that little voice and stopped dead. *Wait a minute,* he thought, *why can't I write that?* And he put it back in. Sukenick experienced a moment of total freedom. *Holy shit!* he thought. *I can write anything I fucking want!* And from that moment on, he did.

This situation, when he wrote the line in question, was something like that one. He didn't know what he meant, but he knew he meant something. He was writing in longhand with a pencil, a nice soft, fat #2 pencil—these things make a difference—and in exasperation dashed off at random a scribble across the page, slammed the notebook closed and tossed it on the desk. Then, *Wait a minute,* he thought, retrieved the book and opening to the page, looked at what he'd just done. *This is what I meant!*

And what he meant, he realized a little later after pondering the line, was what writing was about. It was about freedom. Freedom for the writer and liberation for the reader. Just as Emerson said in his essay "The Poet"—to be free and make free.

Oh he could analyze the line further, just as one might analyze a line from, say T. S. Eliot. It graphed a moment of violent emotion, of quick ups and downs in feeling, of radical instability, he could see that. Moreover, there was a profile in there of Lyndon B. Johnson about whom he had violent feelings because this was written at the height of the Vietnam war. On the other hand it reminded him of the Western landscape he was at about that time learning to know and love, the Badlands of South Dakota, Canyonlands and Arches in Utah, Monument Valley. He could go on and on, just as people did about T. S. Eliot. But the kind of exegesis one might give to someone like John Ashbery, Sukenick felt, would be more appropriate here—that is an analysis that recognizes that the weight of meaning in this case was expressed more formally than usual, or rather, the form was just an extenuation of the content, to paraphrase a cliché.

What it all came to, Sukenick reflected, was that there is such a thing as writing without language, and that, to go further, this writing without language is even a significant part of writing in language—otherwise, why do we have a zillion fonts of print to choose from? The look of writing is part of its meaning. It's part of the argument. Isn't it about time to broaden the frame of reference we're used to in written language to include the range of meaning that graphics can refer to? Isn't this what Pound was really getting at with all his slip-slop about Chinese ideograms? Or e. e. cummings with his page arranged poems? Or even W. C. Williams with his tri-partite foot, reaching to incorporate into written language both the genius of the eye and of the ear, so to ambitiously expand its expressive power? Now, with digitalization of writing via computer, these resources are becoming increasingly obvious. What Sukenick had had to do (and Raymond Federman more so) painstakingly against the grain of the gutenbergian type writer was now, more than facilitated, almost demanded by the resources of the computer if you wanted to exploit the possibilities of the medium.

And the possibilities didn't stop with the visual, they included the sonic. Eventually we were going to have written texts that incorporated sound through digitalization, and not only sound but other senses too. Today's paper has an article about an invention by which you can feel shapes on the computer screen through your mouse. These things are inevitable, but writing will remain the heart—and brain—of the matter. Just as in oratory voice and gesture are important, but you can't do without speech. In writing, graphics is gesture and voice is what you hear with the ear of the mind. And here's the story about Sukenick that I started out to tell. He hears voices. Sometimes they tell him what to write. His first novel, for example, was partly dictated by a voice two inches above his right shoulder. When writing he goes into what some people would call a trance, others a state of meditation. He doesn't think he's unique in this, he's sure it happens to other writers who usually, however, don't put the experience into words or maybe don't consciously register it at all. Because it goes against our rationalist tradition. But, Sukenick believes, there's more than one way to knowledge, and artists have access to alternatives that they arrive at by following the dictates of their medium. In so doing they perform a mediumistic function and keep open lost pathways to knowledge that our modern Western tradition would close. This is what one of Gide's characters means when he advises an aspiring writer to "follow the word." In the same sense that Deep Throat told the Watergate reporters to "follow the money."

When Sukenick goes against the grain, one of his intentions is to expose it. So his idea of the artist as a mediumistic conduit for information not in his control and knowledge beyond his ken opens a broad spectrum of intellectual possibility that reveals our usual empirical take for the narrow bandwidth of knowing which it is. Sukenick doesn't get mystical about this, he's not talking about a direct line to heaven or some spirit world. He's talking about, for example, the voices of the dead as preserved in books, the polyglot babble of community, the abyss of history, the wisdom of babyspeak, the instincts of the body, the realm of the senses, the insight indispensable to research, the influence of place and the weather, the information of animals, the impact of light, the complexities of chance, the gravity of love, the power of eros, the erosions of time, the contortions of pain, the pervasive sadness of death.

Okay, here's the story. One day recently Sukenick was sitting at his desk when he heard a voice telling him,

follow the wind

feel the flow

This was a voice that spoke in whispers. Part of what it said was in images. Sukenick didn't know what the images meant exactly, but they gave him a feeling of intense relief. Oh he could make some guesses—the images suggested flow, wind, clouds, sailing, boats, fish—but it was mostly this sense of relief, release. Maybe that's what they meant. This was a voice that whispered in pictures, and it was telling him he had a bad case of linguistic claustrophobia. As a writer Sukenick was acutely aware that sometimes words separated you from the world—when they're stale or cumbersome or mendacious—and he knew it was the writer's job to play with language so it connected you to the world again. But sometimes he got tired of playing. Then what? Then he knew enough to do something that's basically very frightening to most people: dive into the world beyond language. What? You don't think it's that scary? Imagine walking into a room full of completely unidentifiable objects in a room that's not even a room. Most things in our lives have invisible labels on them, called words, and those that don't we tend not to see. If we stop seeing the invisible labels, or get them mixed up, we're in trouble. Open the pancake. Eat the hammer. Run through the wall.

With all this passing through his mind in a fraction of a second, Sukenick decided the voice was telling him to take a walk, but not along his usual paths, no, but a walk into pure, unlabelled phenomena.

The telephone rang. Sukenick jumped as if he'd been hit by an electric shock. If he'd known it was going to ring he would have turned the phone off. And if he knew who was calling him he wouldn't have answered it.

"Hello, Ron? This is Waldo."

"Hi Waldo."

"How you doing?"

"I'm doing fine. You?"

"Great. I have a new book coming out. I've been hired to write columns for *Details* magazine. And my people are negotiating a contract for a screenplay."

"That is great, Waldo."

"We have to get together. But not till after the weekend. I have an appearance in California and a date with a supermodel who it's very good to be seen with. I'll call as soon as I get back."

"Good Waldo. I look forward to it."

They hung up and Sukenick dropped Waldo into the rich phenomenological soup. Waldo was a phenomenon, a writer who a few years ago was writing only for himself and a few friends. Now his improbable mass market success showed once again the nature of chance and the prospect of freedom it opened in that you might as well do what you want because you never know what's going to happen next.

Sukenick took his hat and coat and went out into the bubbling *Dasein*—he wanted to "be there" so as not to miss anything. But when he got out there it was something like—

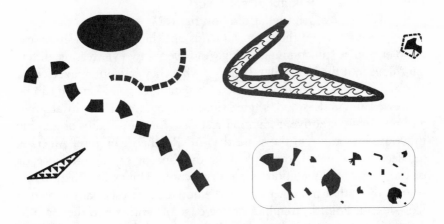

This was, after all, the City. So Sukenick wasn't overly disturbed. An old city-dweller, he knew enough to apply the law of maximal chaos, a law that he himself had written, passed, and enforced at every opportunity. The law of maximal chaos stated simply is that when chaos becomes chaotic enough it turns into a new kind of order. The trick was to wait long enough. And survive.

Sukenick found himself on a pedestrian island at the entrance to the Brooklyn-Battery Tunnel, cars whizzing around him in every direction at a high rate of speed. A rowdy demonstration was going on behind him—placards, chants, cops on horseback. In front of him was some kind of construction project full of jagged holes and pneumatic drills, a huge piledriver hammering metal shafts into the ground, cranes so tall it made him dizzy. A taxicab screeched to a stop right next to him, even though he hadn't hailed it. His painter friend, Hardy, who drove a cab for a living, stuck his head out the window. "Get in!" he screamed over the hellish noise of the street. He got in.

"You looked like you were about to step right into the traffic. What were you thinking?"

"Coincidentally I was thinking about one of your paintings. I was thinking that it was ontically heteronomous."

"What's that mean?" asked Hardy.

"I don't know. I'll have to look it up."

"I think you were having a vatic fit."

"Let's not get mysterious," said Sukenick, "I was just trying to figure out how to talk about your work."

"That's nice. And what did you figure?"

"I mean, even if the painter intends one thing and the viewer sees another, you're still communicating. And even if two viewers see different things in it they can still talk about what they saw and maybe come to some agreement about it. So there's a semantics going on that can be expressed and understood. I figure since your painting is totally abstract and minimally emotive it's a good test case for the validity of graphic thinking. It's brainy in the sense that Ad Reinhardt or Josef Albers is intellectual—it makes you think about the concept, say, of difference, or of the idea of combination as an abstraction. Things like that. While somebody with a more gestural and emotive style, especially someone like Jackson Pollock, trembles on the edge of writing and therefore of written language—in fact you might say that Pollock does a kind of writing without language. Or from another point of view, that of imagery, Miro has worked out something you might call Miro language. While Picasso, with his strong line and special iconography phases into language from both directions. Then you get someone like Cy Twombly who of course crosses frankly from writing into the realm of language with his deployment of words. And once you deploy words you introduce sound because words always imply their sound."

"So what does all this add up to?" asked Hardy.

"It means for one thing writing is a kind of drawing as much as it involves language, and language is a kind of music."

"By coincidence," said Hardy, "I was just on my way to meet Jimmi at the Ear Inn. Want to come?"

"What's with Jimmi?" Jimmi was a jazz musician. Sax.

"Jimmi? Lately he's into singing and writing lyrics. He's working out this interesting idea that while it's obviously true that words, when set to music, are changed by the music, it's equally true that music is changed when lyrics are set to it. In other words, words give a tone and in fact a meaning to the music that it otherwise wouldn't have."

"Really? That has to mean that there's a continuous rhetoric of sound, graphics, and language that's commonly understandable. This may mean nothing to you but it's important. It's important to you as a practicing artist and its important to you if you're interested in taking art on its own terms rather than terms already laid on it by interpreters. The language of art is directly comprehensible by you, without intervention by interpretation, much less theory, just as the language of God is directly receivable by religious fundamentalists. That means no obscure, priestly language is required. Or even wanted. Of course the word may be enriched by interpretation, but it may be impoverished by it too. You could argue that insistent terminological mystification constitutes such an impoverishment. And just gives ammunition to 'creative writing' rednecks and other anti-intellectuals. Though I have to say that intellectuals themselves feed those fires by combining arrogant lip service with profound distrust in their posture—or imposture—regarding the arts. Because they can only admit one way of thinking—theirs, that is, dialectic as opposed to dialogue.

"The point is, all enquote reading of the language of any art is based on the impact of a common rhetoric rather than knowledge of its interpretation. Actually, it would be better to use the word commentary, in a Jewish sense, and distinguish it from the modern sense of interpretation. Commentary doesn't require you establish a meaning for the text, however tentative. Rather, the talmudic tradition of midrash allows and even provokes new departures from the text, taking it as a sort of terminal at which you can stop, embark, or transfer—you may be satisfied with its impact, you may feel the need to take off from it with your own text, or it may remind you of another, apposite or even contradictory text. So the idea is one story leads to another in an ongoing narrative."

Hardy stopped the cab and pushed the meter flag down. "That'll be eight fifty," he said. "You can forget the tip."

"Usually I get paid for lecturing," said Sukenick.

"Here only the cabby gets paid for lecturing. That's why cabbies talk so much."

They were at the Ear Inn over on Spring Street in Soho, a neighborhood that till yuppie-chic moved in was the heart of the art scene and was still something of a crossroads. Basically a grubby bar that serves cheap food and therefore attracts hungry artists, the Ear Inn has history on its side as the second oldest bar in the city, dating back to something like 1812. It's interesting how it got its name, but that's another story. Jimmi was at the bar with a beer.

"You're three beers late," he grouched.

"That should've given you time to mellow out," answered Hardy. Hardy was a shaggy specimen, droopy blond moustache, always in a flannel shirt, jeans, and workboots, and Jimmi was always in some kind of sharp suit with turtleneck, wild well-tended dreadlocks, and skin like oiled mahogany. While separately they were usually easygoing, something about one another's presence made them contentious. They always got into the kind of art arguments that at a certain stage of alcohol consumption risks the possibility of physical confrontation but which nobody can remember the next day. This happened to be the day William Burroughs died. That started it. It was Sukenick who noted the event, quoting Laurence Sterne:

"Whaddyamean!" said Hardy. "All Burroughs did was slap scraps together out of sequence. Everything he got he got from the painters."

"What painters?" Jimmi, his jaw thrusting out.

"The whole tradition of collage, Braque, Picasso, Schwitters, you name it. Not to mention his collagist friend, Brion Gysin."

"I suppose *The Waste Land* and *The Cantos* were copped off Braque?" Sukenick put in.

"It was in the air, in the air," said Hardy. "And we're talking, what, eighty years ago? So I mean Burroughs was hardly an original."

"What about Rauschenberg! What about Rauschenberg! He's still doing it, for chrissake," yelled Jimmi. "Not to mention it was a standard Bebop technique. The Punks call it sampling."

"What's the problem?" butted this dark, goodlooking big woman in striped bib overalls. "Sounds like you boys are ready to duke it out." Actually, Rose, a major installation artist, could probably put any one of them away and they all knew it. She always insisted she wasn't named after the flower but after the past tense of rise.

"We're talking about collage," Hardy said.

"Collage is out," said Rose. "Finished. Mosaic is in."

"What's the difference?"

"Collage deals with disparate parts. It marks the transition from Modern to Postmodern. Mosaic takes disparate parts and turns them into new wholes. It's the beginning of something else."

"Is that the slogan for the day?" asked Hardy.

"Want to make something of it?" said Rose. She crooked her arm and made a muscle, then she made a fist with her other hand and brought it down on the inside of her elbow.

Hardy raised a hand with middle finger extended.

Jimmi exchanged a high five with Rose.

Sukenick saluted them all and ordered a round of brewskis. Things quieted down for a while. The bar was rather crowded for late afternoon. There were still some late lunch eaters at the paper-covered tables but the after work drinkers were starting to straggle in, and there were also a lot of people who looked like they didn't have any schedule at all perched on the tacky red plastic-covered stools at the long wooden bar. Buxom blond waitresses in tight t-shirts tended the tables. A soundless TV hanging from the ceiling showed an ice hockey game and the sound system was playing country and rock. Ancient looking crap photos and posters cluttered the walls and even the low wooden ceiling. On the wall demarking the front from the back room there was a big official sign that said DO NOT TIE UP AT THIS PIER—DEPT. OF PORTS, no doubt in memory of a time when the bar was actually on the pre-landfilled waterfront. On the wall around from the sign was a six foot high wooden ear.

Rose started talking about her latest project, an entire apartment with walls made of video screens, each showing ongoing images from different TV news programs. She said it was part of her "Reality" series.

"Because that's what our reality is," she said.

"You don't believe that," said Hardy.

"Why would she say it if she don't believe it?" challenged Jimmi.

"It's a put-on," insisted Hardy.

"Wait a minute," said Sukenick. "Wait a minute, wait a minute, let me get this." He pulled a small tape recorder from his jacket pocket and turned it on.

Sukenick: Okay, who's to say what's real and what's not?

Hardy and Rose, speaking at the same time: Who asked he she what your opinion are we talking about?

Jimmi: No, no. Because it's the wrong question. What do you expect? You ask the wrong question you get the wrong answer.

Rose: You can ask any question you damn please, I don't have to answer it.

Sukenick: No, but wait a minute . . .

Hardy: What are we talking about?

Rose: How the fuck do I know, I didn't bring it up.

Sukenick: No, wait a minute, wait a minute . . .

Jimmi: I want another beer, can I get another beer please?

Sukenick: No, wait a minute, the important thing is [sound of beer being drawn, crescendo of background conversation, a woman yelling "Sally, Sally," a drunken male voice singing "Mack the Knife."]

Rose: What?

Hardy: What you're getting at is images. Right? *The Society of the Spectacle*. Right? The Situationists were right on the money. *Détournement*. Read *Lipstick Traces*. By whatsisname.

Sukenick: Greil Marcus.

Hardy: Use it against them. Turn their own shit against them, that's the ticket.

Jimmi: Fuckin A.

Rose: Excuse me. Excuse me. Do I get to say anything about it, I mean it is my piece.

Jimmi: Sure, go right ahead baby. You got the floor.

Rose: The reason I call it "Reality" is because I don't mean reality.

Jimmi: No? Whaddya mean?

Rose: Unreality. I mean I'm trying to tell the truth. That's a different kettle of fish.

Hardy: The Kettle of Fish used to be a nice bar in the Village.

Rose: Art is a discipline of truth, not reality.

Sukenick: Kerouac used to hang out there.

Jimmi: Where?

Sukenick: The Kettle. A rough place. He almost got killed there one night. Outside. Corso told me about it.

Hardy: Can you have one without the other?

Sukenick: One what?

Hardy: Truth and reality.

Rose: Excuse me, that's the whole point. I don't know beans about reality. I mean what the fuck is reality? I just try to tell the truth.

Hardy: How do you know if it's true if you don't know it's real?

Jimmi: Touché, man, touché.

Rose: You argue.

Sukenick: Well you came to the right place.

Jimmi: It's true if you got it on tape. Ain't that true, man?

Sukenick: No. It's just real. Real to reel. But it may not be true.

Hardy: Am I supposed to take this conversation seriously? I mean is this just bar talk or what?

Sukenick: Don't forget a whole esthetic movement came out of talk in these bars. A whole series of esthetic movements that changed the culture. From the Abstract Expressionists in the San Remo to Andy Warhol in Max's Kansas City and on and on.

Jimmi: That's right. And Sukenick's the man who wrote the book, I read it. *Down and In, Life in the Underground.* That's it. All those tape recordings he did in the bars. That's about us.

Hardy:	Oh yeah. Who's us?
Jimmi:	Us. We're the guys the academics need to study.
Rose:	Not any more. Now they study one another.
Jimmi:	Give em a break. They got to get their shit straightened out.
Rose:	You guys sound like a bunch of lawyers arguing.
Jimmi:	No we're not. We're arguing like artists.
Rose:	What's the difference?
Jimmi:	We start out by arguing and we end up by dancing.
Sukenick:	Or by fighting.
Jimmi:	Same thing. Kind of fights we have there are no winners no losers.
Hardy:	Right. We fight for the fun of it. And to work out our issues. Fighting is just a sublimation of arguing.
Jimmi:	Hey, you got that bass ackwards kiddo.
Hardy:	What do you sing when you're coming back from Jersey on the George Washington Bridge?
Rose (singing):	Bridge Washington George.
Jimmi:	Buy that lady a beer!
Hardy:	Hey Sukenick, how about rewinding the tape and letting us hear what we said?
Jimmi:	Yeah, let's hear how stupid we sound.

But just at that point Eddy came in and Sukenick turned off the recorder because he always found Eddy long winded. He always got caught up in his own stories and went round and round till you lost track of time.

"You'll never believe what just happened to me," said Eddy, without even saying hello.

"Okay," said Hardy, "go on."

"I was walking across the north side of Washington Square when this guy in a fedora and a cigarette dangling out of his mouth almost bumps into me. At first I thought he was going to try and sell me some pot, you know what it's like around there, but he excuses himself and then just as I'm walking away he grabs my arm.

'Hey wait a minute,' he says.

'Yeah?' I say.

'You some kind of writer or painter? or maybe a musician?'

'Yeah, so?'

'Well nothing, except I was wondering what happened to them all. Place used to be crawling with them, doncha know, now all I see around here is students, reefer heads, and professors. So what are you, a writer maybe?'

I took a good look at him. He was an old guy, but spry, wire rim glasses, and not too nutty looking for a nut. 'I'm a performance artist.'

'A performance artist, what's that?'

Well I thought he was putting me on so I start to walk away, but he grabs my arm again. 'No, really,' he says, 'I've been away a long while, doncha know. A performance artist, huh, that sounds good, is that the new thing? Like vaudeville, maybe?'

'It's quite popular, as I'm sure you know. I sort of act things out on stage.'

'Well don't that sorta put the kaibosh on the acting profession?'

'Why, are you an actor?'

'I used to be a writer, now I mostly do water colors. My name is Henry Miller, maybe you've heard of me.'

'Henry Miller's been dead for years.'

'You don't have to tell me that.'

I decide to humor the nut, I figured maybe he'd have an interesting shtick. 'What are you doing around here?'

'Oh, I was having my penis stretched.'

'By some charming lady, I hope.'

'No, by a doctor. Penis enlargement treatments.'

'You have problems in that direction?'

'No, not at all, but I think everybody should be as big as possible, doncha know.'

Actually, this story was starting to sound familiar. I'd once heard from a woman who was married to the son of Henry Miller's doctor, who had a practice on Washington Square, that he once gave Henry Miller penis enlargement treatments. I figured the guy must have heard the same story.

'If you don't mind my saying so,' I tell him, 'I think it's funny that a guy who writes so much about his sex exploits gets penis enlargement treatments.'

'I was never a sex writer. I know everybody thinks that but it's a mistake. I was just writing autobiography as fiction, that was the interesting thing, I mean not veiled autobiography but real autobiography, using myself as a character and all. Because the self, doncha see, is the richest body of data you'll ever know. And even those stories were embroidered of course, especially the sex stories, I mean it's an old American male form of oratory—bragging. It's just talk, buddy, good old bar room talk. Didn't anybody ever hear of the tall story? That's the point, doncha know.'

'So you're saying you're not a sex writer? Then what kind of writer are you?'

'Looking back on it, I'd say I was a religious writer.'

'How's that?'

'Yeah, a religious writer, I'd say that fits the bill. I wrote sermons. Another old American oratorical form. And the sermons were about salvation. That's what my books were about. Salvation. You can change your life. What could be more American than that? I really struck a chord there, doncha know. If you'd spent any real time in Europe you'd realize how American that is. You grow up in France, Italy, wherever, you're stuck with what you're born into. But in the old U S of A it's different, and you can really see it from over there. That's why I only hit my stride when I got to Paris. In America you can be born again. Shit, you can be born any number of times. No matter how much I hated the nightmare of American puritanism, no matter how much I loved the cultivation of the French, I went there, yes, I went, I fled, I escaped to Europe to fulfill an American dream. You can change your life. You can see the light. You can be saved. Hallelujah! Come unto me and you shall be saved. Come unto me and read my book and the book shall save you. You shall be saved from the air conditioned nightmare. You shall be saved from an inhumane puritanism. You shall be saved from a diabolic materialism. You shall see the truth and it shall make you free. Hallelujah! Hallelujah! Hallelujah! That's the mission of art in America. In Europe art is an extension of the good life, it's an esthetic practice. Fuck that. In America art makes you free.'

'So why are you doing water colors now instead of writing?'

'Because one day you wake up and realize you've said all you got to say, and you go on to something else, doncha know. It's not the particular art that's important, it's not art at all. It's the spirit, brother, it's the holy spirit. Without it art is dead, with it garbage collecting can be alive.'

"So, like, how do you like it?" asked Eddy.

"Like what?" asked Hardy.

"My new performance piece, stupid."

"Well, bravo, I guess. What else is new?"

"I liked the part about the rhetoric of preaching," said Sukenick.

"Rhetoric? I didn't say anything about rhetoric."

"Rhetoric is Sukenick's thing for the day," said Hardy.

"It's true that's what I'm thinking about today, tomorrow I'll probably think something different. But what I think about preaching is that rhetoric can make us come together, in community, in communion like preachers do, as well as make us contentious, like lawyers do."

"Well ain't that nice," said Jimmi. "Only I'm not so sure I want to come together with Hardy. Now if you can arrange for me to come together with Rose, that's a different story."

"Fat chance," said Rose.

"Everybody's got to develop his own rhetoric of seduction," said Sukenick.

"Jesus, come off it already," said Hardy.

"That was a true story, by the way," said Eddy.

"Whaddya mean," said Jimmi, "you met the real ghost of Henry Miller?"

"How do you define a real ghost?" asked Sukenick.

"No, I mean, that was my interpretation of Henry Miller and I think it's true."

"You do impressions now?" asked Rose.

"No," said Hardy, "what it was was, Eddy met this other performance artist practicing his Henry Miller impression."

"We all have our acts," said Rose. "We're all characters in our own stories. Except for me. I'm genuine. The real me."

"Come on, you're the biggest character around here," said Jimmi. "Ask anyone."

"Oh yeah?" said Rose. "Let me tell you what happened to me once. I was working on a piece when I fell off a ladder on my head. I was okay but I couldn't remember anything. I could remember falling off the ladder but that was about all. This was at a time when I was really blocked, I couldn't produce anything I liked. Everything

I did seemed too arty to me. I looked around my loft and said what is this shit, did I do this? Before I had a chance to think about it I went around and changed everything and it was great. I really couldn't remember anything, like I couldn't even remember what I'd been doing two minutes ago much less two months ago, but who gave a fuck. I liked it. A lot. After a while this guy comes in, very handsome. I didn't recognize him but I didn't say anything. I was very attracted to him, I wanted to make love with the dude. He must have gotten the message because before I knew it I was in bed with him. Wow, what a stud. I had a great orgasm and with that my memory came back. I was so disappointed, this guy was my boy friend who I'd decided was the biggest jerk in the world and was about to dump. But lemme tell you, I took a look at the art I'd done while I was amnesiac and I still thought it was great. Just like I had to admit that making love to the dude was great when I could screw him without all our history, because it was just the moment."

"So what is this supposed to prove?" asked Hardy.

"Beats me," said Rose. "I forgot what I was trying to prove."

"You were trying to prove you're the real you, and what it proves is that the real you only lives in the present, when you come right down to it," said Sukenick. "And therefore real art can only be made in the present, maximal thought minimal memory, otherwise it gets arty. Like, academics need more memory but artists need faster modems. Which explains why you still liked it after the fact, though that was only an afterthought."

"Like jazz," said Jimmi. "All you can do is record it. If you fuck with the recording too much after the fact it's a mess. Better to record it all over again."

"Let me tell you a story about that," said Hardy. "This is another true story. One time, see, I was floating down the river on a marble slab . . ."

But the place was getting noisy now with the chat and laughter of the afterwork crowd and you couldn't hear what Hardy was saying. They had moved away from the bar and were approximately in front of the big wooden—or was it tin?—ear. The noise level of the sound system was up, the crowd was getting collectively drunk, everybody was talking and nobody was listening.

"The bottom line," Sukenick yelled into the big ear, he was drunk now, "is that art, any kind of art, even the evillest art, is good

98

for you. It's even good for you when it's bad for you, it's best for you when it's bad for you. Because it wakes up your soul. And it's not even art, it's pure consciousness, *moksha*."

But the big ear didn't give any sign that it heard him. In fact what they were playing on the sound system was soul, and in one corner a couple started dancing, and then three couples were dancing in the chaos of the bar, and it seemed to be contagious because soon almost everybody was dancing, even Sukenick was dancing with Rose, around and around, dizzy and thinking it's happening, time is curving, the stream is eddying, the current is slowing and it's all moving downstream like a river with no shores, endless

What's Watts

Rodia woke up late that morning. He had a hangover. He was thinking about his red Hudson touring car. His much quoted comment that he wanted to do something in the United States because there are nice people in this country explains nothing. Or if it explains something it is not what it is supposed to explain. This is a documentary. But the problem with it as documentary is that there are not enough facts. And such facts as there are are not the right facts. That is to say they don't explain what you want explained. They explain something else. What you do in such a case is you either explain something else or you explain nothing at all but if you explain nothing at all what is the sense of writing a documentary? However, that is the trouble with documentary there are never enough facts. You begin with the impression that if you have enough facts you can explain everything but in fact each fact you uncover requires another fact in explanation so that in a certain large sense and I think experience in the exact sciences will bear this out the more you know the less you know. Civilization then drives toward ignorance you sneer. Nevertheless I must answer in the positive. Ignorance in the sense that Adam was ignorant before the apple. As the fish is ignorant of its water. As the mind is ignorant of its next thought. And perhaps this is the key to Rodia.

An uneducated Italian laborer settles in a then rural area of Los Angeles and working completely by himself for thirty-three years constructs one of America's major art works a series of towers ten stories high. When he is finished he gives the whole thing to a neighbor and disappears apparently to die. These are the hard facts of the story which everyone knows. His name was Sabatino Rodia. Or

Simone Rodia. Or Simon Rodilla. Or Sam Rodia. El Italiano. The rural area of Los Angeles became a Mexican section of the city and then became Watts. The more you know the less you know. The facts are a little unstable. There are anecdotes which could imply anything. Here is a snapshot of Rodia thumbing through a book on Gaudi. A little old man at the end of his life he has been persuaded to come to Berkeley and listen to a lecture on his towers. He listens with detached interest. It is as if someone were giving a lecture on his wife who had died years ago before he started the towers. Yes she was beautiful yes he loved her yes he still misses her so what. He once said he wanted to do something big that people would remember him by. When he left the towers he left them to be vandalized by neighborhood kids and torn down by city bureaucrats so what. There were thirty-three years of his life in the towers but now everything was finished. So what so what so what. He did not want to think about his wife. He did not want to think about the towers. He did not want to think about his life being over. They had compared him to Gaudi. At the end of the lecture he asked to see some pictures of the things by Gaudi. "This man," he was supposed to have asked, "he had helpers?" When answered in the affirmative he said, "I never had no help at all."

As I was saying perhaps ignorance is the key. We all of course know what's going to happen next. Only artists don't know what's going to happen next a quirk of ignorance they share with history and the weather. This is the key quirk of the quirky mind that produces the work of the artist. Rodia did not know that day in 1921 that sunny Los Angeles day that he was going to dig a hole in his back yard and bury his beautiful red Hudson touring car. If you had asked him afterward why he did it he wouldn't have known. He didn't do it for a reason. He would have made up a story. It was a story. Stories don't have reasons. Or if they have them they have them after the fact like the weather. Then the reasons become part of the story. The mind is like the weather and this is the reason that everyone likes a good story.

Rodia woke up late that morning. He had a hangover. The Hudson was a seed. A metal seed Rodia planted in his yard. Inside the seed was his whole life up to then. This was the life he was burying. Rodia didn't know his life was a seed. He was conducting a funeral. He was burying his life. One part of his life was over. He woke up late in the morning with a hangover and he knew that part of his life was over. He washed his mouth with a swallow of warm beer and took his spade into the yard. It took him four days to dig the hole and another day to bury the car in it. The following spring the towers began to grow.

Divide

It began when the C.I.A. contacted my publisher and asked for a copy of my last novel. At first I thought it was funny. What would the C.I.A. do with an off-beat novel that even most of the critics couldn't understand? I was flattered, in a way, for the attention. I asked the publisher if they were sure it wasn't the International Communications Agency, the I.C.A., which runs international cultural events for the government. No, it was the C.I.A., and the publisher hadn't sent the book because they hadn't sent payment for it. I thought I might send them a signed copy, compliments of the author, with a jocular dedication. "Flattered that you find my work Central, Yours . . ."; "From one who also works for the Intelligence, Fraternally . . ."; "We are all Agents, Subversively . . ."

Then suddenly it wasn't so funny. Absurd, perhaps. Inexplicable. Maybe somebody up there with a literary bent heard about the book by word-of-mouth and just wanted a freebie, pure literary curiosity. Gordon Liddy, maybe? While it was true that the President had just authorized the C.I.A. to engage in domestic intelligence again, I couldn't believe that included literary intelligence. Maybe they'd concluded my novel is a secret code. I mean, my work is not for everyone. Still who knows what might be considered political these days? Possibly the very fact my work is not for everyone was considered political. Maybe I was considered an "elitist." Maybe, for all I knew, they liked the fact that I was an elitist. Maybe they were going to try to recruit me. Didn't the very fact that they neglected to include payment with their book order imply a certain complicity, as if they could expect everybody's cooperation?

Expect cooperation. That, on the other hand, seemed a little menacing. Nonsense, I was just letting my imagination run on. But what did they expect? What did they think an imaginative writer was going to do with this kind of occult event? Forget about it? The C.I.A. asks for one of your books just like that, for no reason at all, and you're supposed to forget about it? Or maybe I wasn't supposed to forget about it. Maybe I was doing just what they wanted me to do. Get paranoid. Be aware they had their eye on me. Involve myself in endless speculation about their motives. Maybe I'm in effect collaborating with them already, despite myself and without knowing it. It is not totally impossible that the whole point of all this is to get me to write C.I.A. stories. And what would be their motive for that? Why, to help make everyone aware of their presence of course, but in a subtle, oblique way, nothing heavy handed or threatening, nothing to chill the atmosphere, just a quiet reminder that they are there, invisible, occult, omnipotent, there.

But of course, this is all ridiculous. The whole incident—is it an "incident" already?—is no doubt completely innocent. I was making molehills out of goose bumps. The C.I.A. has a right to read novels too, just like any other citizen. And any citizen has the right to express suspicion. Who could be that suspicious of me, I wondered. And for what, since I am completely innocent. Innocent? Of what? Who mentioned anything about being guilty of something? That's not even a consideration. Surely the message implied in this affair, if there is a message and it is an affair, is nothing more serious than "Be careful," a warning that could be considered as much a favor as a threat. Thanks.

I understood very well what was happening to me. As usual my imagination had seized on the murky data of experience and had made of it a continuation of my writing. But understanding it didn't necessarily mean I could do anything about it. My life was an endless short story whose episodes derived as much from the unpredictable currents of my mind as from the dark flood of experience. The best cure for this mood was sunshine, especially the hard clear Colorado sunlight shining outside which did not permit the ambiguities of chiaroscuro to obscure the sharp snowpeaks of the Continental Divide that I could see from my window, fourteen thousand feet of pure fact sawing into the steel blue sky.

I put on my down jacket and walked to a trailhead at the edge of town. From there it was a short, steep hike up through a deep slot into the first pinnacles of the Rockies to a high rampart that gave a clear, far view of both the jagged line of the Front Range and the Great Plains receding sixty miles into the blue distance in the direction of Chicago. Perspective. It was one of the virtues of living on the Divide. Perspective and schizophrenia. The shopping plazas at the east side of town were populated by heavy, dish faced farmers and grey suited businessmen, while the bars on the western edge had a clientele of mountain men with fleas in their beards, local cowboys in down vests and hip bachelors with styled hair and clothes like Southern California. But the geography here suited me, on the blade edge of America. Having been raised in New York and having lived a long time in California, it seemed just right that I should end up on the Continental Divide. When I lived in New York I used to feel paranoid about the unleashed libido of California and when I lived in California I used to feel persecuted by the grey power centers of the east. Now I could look in both directions and by a slight shift in sensibility or location feel part of either. The best cure for paranoia is schizophrenia.

Somewhere between my cowboy boots and my Brooklyn head I had made my accommodation to the Sun Belt. In my mind, by moving to the Southwest I had finally become an American. New York was not America, it was New York, and in Los Angeles it was easy to see oneself as the offspring of immigrants finally arrived in the promised land, cosmopolite in utopia. But as in Paris when your interior monologue imperceptibly switches to French, out here—I could still think of it as "out here"—I was beginning to catch myself thinking in Cowboy: "A short ways up the trail here an ah kin see the tall buildins in Dinver." And I could, from a distance of thirty miles horizontal and a half a mile vertical, which always gave me a small shock since, where I came from, you looked from the tall buildings down at everything else, not down from anything else at the tall buildings. Yup, out here I had finally become one of us, spelled U.S. That is, until this casual gesture by the C.I.A.—if the C.I.A. made any casual gestures—placed the edge of the wedge in the fault of my contained schizophrenia, the fault being an old paranoia native to the alien coasts. The Americans are after me again.

I was on a pinnacle just under the crest of the first wall of the mountains, the Divide stretching from my view north to Wyoming. Way down below I saw the town pooling in a bowl of the plains, the red sandstone and green grass of the campus and, with my binoculars,

I could pick out my house. On a mesa rising out of the plains beyond a low line of hills I could look down at the modernist castle of the National Center for Atmospheric Research and, ten miles south, on the next mesa over, at the neat metallic spread of the Rocky Flats nuclear plant where all the plutonium triggers for all the atom bombs in America are produced. People who bought houses around here had to sign a statement that they knew they were living in a ten mile radius of Rocky Flats. There was a town downwind whose water supply had been contaminated by radioactivity.

But radioactivity was not what I thought about when I thought about Rocky Flats, and here comes my paranoia again, what I thought about was the last war, and by the last war I meant the next one, and the certainty that one of the first Russian bombs to drop would drop on Rocky Flats and goodbye. That was a circumstance that had its advantages as well as its disadvantages though, and here comes schizophrenia to the rescue, since if it meant that folks around here would be among the first to go, who would want to be around afterward anyway? Nevertheless, there was a bumper sticker popular in the area that read, "Close Rocky Flats As A Nuclear Bomb Plant," and there was usually more than one demonstration a year at the plant, often including civil disobedience, with attendance at times numbering in the tens of thousands. One of these I had myself attended. Did they know? Was that it? Did they know, for that matter, that I sometimes came up here and sometimes trained my binoculars on the place?

But I was tired of thinking about Rocky Flats. I had come up here to get away from all that. From my pinnacle there was a narrow ridge slicing off behind me toward the higher cliffs. When I say narrow I mean a razor edge of about a foot of rock with an occasional stunted pine growing out of it and a straight drop of about five hundred feet on either side. I had never tried walking across it and I knew I shouldn't but I decided to anyway. One of the problems of climbing around in the mountains is that I tend to get overexhilarated by the altitude. It's a physiological effect of the thinning air, like getting drunk. The higher you get the higher you get. I find myself doing things that my better judgment tells me I should never do alone, leaping from rock to rock like a goat in places where any slight accident that prevented me from getting back down out of the mountains would mean death by exposure. But I wanted to escape my fears of civilization. I prefer fear of nature. I figure I can make it across the ridge if I'm real careful, go slow and use hand holds at the scarier parts. On the other side I can see a break in the cliff through which it looks like I can climb all the way to the crest. From there I might be able to get a glimpse of the family of golden eagles I had seen above the peaks once, playing in the updrafts.

I start picking my way along the ridge trying not to look down the sides of the drop, looking down makes me feel like my rectum is failing out. I'm sure that if I can get across here safely I'll be able to get back down the same way. I don't know much about rock climbing but I know one thing they say is that it's always harder to get down than to get up. Several people a year get stranded up here, sometimes because of a sudden change in the weather which happens frequently, and some just because they find it's a lot harder to get down. Some try, some die. Some stay put and are gotten out by the local mountain rescue team if their absence is discovered before they freeze to death, which can happen in a few hours, depending on the weather, and if they can be located. Some are found years later, their skeletons matched up with the missing persons roster by their bridgework. Half way up the incline of the ridge I stop to rest. It's steeper than I thought and my heart is pounding from the exertion and the altitude. Behind me now the plains and mesas are out of sight, all I can see are the pine covered foothills.

I hear a slight thrashing noise and in the ravine below me I discover a mule deer making its way through the trees. I get my binos on it, a pretty good sized buck working its antlers through the dense pine branches. For a moment it seems trapped, then shaking its head violently, breaks free and disappears down a gully. At that moment, following the abrupt movement of the deer with my binos, I become disoriented, and trying to refocus as I drop the binos from my eyes, get dizzy, lose my balance, and start an odd dance on my rock perch that seems to take place in slow motion as I try to prevent myself from falling. Falling. Then fall, for an instant totally out of control, to land just below my rock on a patch of dirt at the edge of the big drop, safe but nearly blanking out, and with the bizarre sensation that someone is watching me. Who?

The thought fills my mind for a fraction of a second, then evaporates. Someone watching me? I put it down to altitude inebriation, get up carefully, take a few deep breaths and head on up the spine of the ridge. From here on it rose at a steep angle, and though I practically have to crawl up the last fourth of its length I make it across without further trouble. But when I stop to look back from the other side I'm amazed at what I just climbed. The ridge seems to drop off into space and disappear like the tip of a knife. Up ahead, though, it still looks like I can make it through the cliffs to the top. Except I would have to hurry, because it's getting a little late in the day.

Behind the first cliff the way opens out unexpectedly into a wide snowy field, still sloped steeply, but that allows me to climb much faster. Here again, even though I can see for quite a distance behind me, I have the feeling of being watched, even followed. It puzzles me, I'm already frightened of the mountains and it raises the level of dread like water filling a sink. Irrationally, it makes me climb faster than I should to conserve my energy, panting up toward the opening in the next line of cliffs. I reach a kind of steep gully and begin scrambling up over icy boulders, realizing I'm not wearing the right shoes for this kind of climbing, I have on boots, but not cleated hiking boots. Am I trying to get away? And if so, from what? Then all at once I understand that to be followed I don't have to be followed by somebody. Or something. It's utterly possible just to be followed, as simple as that. By what? By nothing, or by everything. Just to have the experience of being followed and, correspondingly, the impulse to escape, to get away, and why not? I recognize for the first time that it's not only me, that everyone is followed, that it has become the fundamental condition of our lives, that we think we are being followed by this agent, or that organization, or such and such bureaucracy, while the fact is we are being followed by history itself in the form of various agencies but sometimes more diffusely as a huge, pervasive presence, like a terminal disease, like a mass grave, like drowned voices, like that genre of absolute shock beyond pity of which we must speak but about which there is nothing to say.

I'm climbing a kind of chimney now where the gully has narrowed to a steep ascent of about sixty degrees. The sky has greyed over and it's getting cold. I'm not wearing warm enough clothing for this kind of weather. Reaching the top of the chimney in a state of extreme fatigue and chill, I look around for some kind of shelter. I had heard about the dangers of hypothermia and know I should have brought something to eat. I'm on an immense, up-tilted rock shelf, bare of trees or bushes. From there I can see it's begun to snow on the peaks to the north like heavy grey curtains descending from a grey sky. I know that as soon as it starts snowing here it's going to be impossible to get down. As I start climbing toward the ridge, hoping for a cave, the wind starts gusting, and before I have a chance even to arrive at the top it begins to snow. I settle behind some boulders to wait out the blinding, wind driven storm, but even from the shelter of the rocks it's impossible to see. The air is a white sheet, a blank page. And it's freezing. Nothing could survive in this kind of environment, I think, not even the animals. They had been happy at first in the preserve, or so we thought, but it soon became ambiguous as to whether the barbed wire was meant to keep them out or us in, or even as to who was "us" and who was "them." We thought of us as ourselves and the animals, living together inside, but we could get out and the animals couldn't. Outside they had weapons and some kind of vague, lethal teleology. There was mounting pressure on us to leave. We were given assurances that the animals would be taken care of, and so finally we left. But stories began to filter out, like the instant slaughter of whole herds of elephants with automatic weapons and anti-tank rockets. And so we came back. We found the animals starving and diseased, penned up in an ever smaller perimeter of barbed wire, and yet the wire was their only defense against even greater obscenity. We resolved then to stay and do all we could to protect and save the preserve. The animals were upset but still innocent, nevertheless our supporters gradually dropped away and deserted us. They came at the moment we were stripped of support. They had tanks and troop carriers. They cut the barbed wire. The animals looked on, wide-eyed, apprehensive, numb, a rhino, two hippos, something with fluted horns, the cats hiding in the bush. We jumped into the muddy gap through the wire, blocking the way. Nobody is going to come through here, we said, taking our stand in the mud. We were nude. There were three of us, our bodies cut and scarred. We knew what they wanted to do and we told them they weren't going to do it. Because, we said, men can't do that. We repeated this three times. Then the dream panned across our three pale, rigid bodies. Each of us, one with a stump, one with a lumpy scar, one with a jagged incision, had had his penis cut off.

Death On the Supply Side

The Church of San Clemente in Rome is not far from the Coliseum. I had been there twenty-four years ago and now, in Rome for the first time since, I have a strong impulse to visit it again, I don't know why. The church consists of three levels: the upper church at street level was built at the beginning of the twelfth century, the lower church beneath it is from the fourth century, and sixty feet underground, next to the remnant of a palazzo from the first century, is an ancient Mithraic temple. It's this temple that pulls me back, that seems to retain some kind of magnetism for me across the years since my first visit. All I remember of it is darkness, a white altar, and the sound of water. And a certain feeling of quiescence and awe.

For several years I've had the desire to come back to Rome, for reasons obscure to my imagination. But I have learned to follow my nose in matters of the imagination, which some times requires its peculiar forms of research.

Now that I'm in Rome I don't like it much. It's a miscellaneous clutter of disordered rubble blackened by the smog that also makes it hard to breathe. In Rome you get high culture at its worst, detached from any communal matrix and on display, basically, for a price to those who can pay. What's most evident in the monuments and ruins is a history of voracious looting and scavenging, culture feeding on itself in a progressive comedy of transformation, the spoils of conquest ornamenting the Roman Empire, Roman columns used to build Christian churches, Romanesque frescos ripped off for Baroque buildings, the Pantheon robbed to decorate St. Peter's, antique monuments as marble quarries for newer palazzi. From my window I can see the trashed jumble of the Roman Forum, most of the remaining columns and arches wrapped in plastic net and scaffolding against the miasmic smog.

But there's also something vivacious about this jungle of stone, its ongoing cultural cannibalism resembling the vitality of an ecosystem that survives and flourishes by feeding on itself, every loss representing also a gain. Besides, I happen to be well set-up to take advantage of Rome. A friend has loaned me an apartment in the Trastevere, one of the more sympathetic sections of the city, and one which—higher than the smog-dense center and somewhat peripheral—is a bit less polluted by the industrio-vehicular miasma. My only obligation is to pay the cleaning lady and take care of the horse that comes with the apartment. The latter is no problem, since the apartment is large and the horse has her own room, and the problems of feeding and elimination are much facilitated by an adjacent dumbwaiter. Of course I have to take her out twice a day, but there are, after all, other horses occasionally in the streets of the Trastevere, and my speckled, white, black-maned little mare is no big deal to the locals. The only problem is that she seems to be sick, or pining away, or both, maybe for my friend, but I know my friend isn't coming back, so what can I do?

Every day I go out and do the tourist thing, persisting till I can no longer tolerate the miasma which gives me a sore throat and headache, and even affects my lungs. Tell your tourist friends to avoid Rome till they do something to clean it up. When I tell you the miasma is severe and a public scandal I am not exaggerating. This year the police began wearing gas masks as on-the-job protection, but had to discard them because of enforcement of an obscure law against wearing masks in public, exhumed by the city's image guardians.

Bit by bit I get to know once more Rome's tourist attractions, oddly avoiding San Clemente, which I think of, when I think of it at all, with both anticipation and dread. In fact I don't think about it much, any more than I do about my slowly dying mother back in the States. Sooner or later I know I'll have to think about it, why think about it till then? When you have a premonition of feelings you suspect are like a land mine set to go off, you're not eager to step on the mine. My characteristic emotional tactics seem to be to angle in on things, allowing time for the substrate to settle into place so that it can support the changing superstructures of consciousness. This is probably a mode inherited from my mother, who never faced anything consciously at all, period.

My father, on the contrary, was an emotional bull, abrupt and blunt, who as a result often missed the meaning of things, maybe even, when he died, the meaning of his own death. Yet, meaningless or not, his stubborn decisiveness produced a sense of authority, which means something after all.

Down on the corner of Mameli and Tittoni the man with no arms and no legs sits in his wheel chair. Today he seems to be wearing a suit. A young man comes over, puts a cigarette in his mouth and lights it for him. This citizen, though limbless, manages to project a sense of macho self-confidence that is, to say the least, surprising. Tanned and bald as a bocce ball, bull neck, Roman nose, authoritarian jaw, he perches in his wheelchair with his pants folded under his trunk in a way that outlines what looks like a pair of oyster specials, jumbo jewels, muchos cojones, big ballocks, in a word, balls. When pretty girls walk by he sings them songs in a loud baritone that hurries them along flushed and angry. His act always leaves me wondering how many women in fantasy might remember a man with a single member.

This man, Signor Cranio, as I come to call him, never lacks company. There's always somebody talking to him, somebody to wheel him into the sun, which he seems to prefer, someone to put on or take off his rather dashing straw hat. He evidently exercises a kind of fascination on the neighborhood, capitalizing on his dismemberment, chatting and joking endlessly, his only tool his tongue. But then, he has a neighborhood to fascinate, friends, acquaintances, undoubtedly nearby relatives, a network of support. I hate to think of the fate of a quadruple amputee in the States, isolated, the family working for remote branches of the national corporation to make its buck, dumped in one of the government death factories, also known as nursing homes. It's part of a system that masks a basic cruelty with a sanctimonious kindness.

When I get back to the States I'll find my mother in a nursing home, permanently bed-ridden, where she's to be sent from the hospital. It might have been better if she'd gone out on the operating table, but she seems to have a native vitality that keeps her going however impaired, unluckily for her. I'm not sure when I'll have to go back. Every time the phone rings late at night I'm hit with a shot of dread.

It looks like Signor Cranio may be a drug drop. Every morning a big balding guy in a seedy suit sidles up to him in an ostentatiously nonchalant way, looks around with a display of innocence, and slips something in Signor Cranio's jacket pocket. Sometime during the morning one of a variety of men strolls up and slides whatever it is out of the pocket, slipping something else into the other pocket. Whereupon a few minutes later the first guy ambles around the comer, pulls whatever it is out of that pocket, puts it in his own, and rambles down the street with a slow, self-satisfied strut. The Trastevere has been one of the drug zones of Rome, and the park on the hill above my apartment contains many bushes behind which suspicious-looking people are having ambiguous encounters. I wonder if the Mafia is present here with its discipline of silence and omertá. If so Signor Cranio would seem a lousy bet since all he can do is talk and sing.

Rome is filled with ambiguous auguries, ominous event. A friend is immobilized in an auto accident, another has a spasm of spontaneous paralysis. The city is filled with tombs and catacombs, mausoleums, sarcophagi and cemeteries, the detritus of dead civilizations, morbid emblems of the Christians' dying god, old women mumbling to moribund priests, an architecture of rotting magnificence, decay and miasma, scored by vespa buzz and deisel fart. The cult of Mithras was based on blood rites cultivating loyalty and terror, reflecting the god's slaying of the sacred bull of evil. It appealed especially to the Roman Legions. It probably would have appealed to the Mafia. Mithras was a Zoroastrian religion whose wide-open struggle between good and evil for a time rivalled Christianity's promise of submission and salvation. Be a good boy. For Mithras the threat of evil, the terror of death are tempered by the cult of loyalty. Hang tough. All we have is one another. The Romans are nice to one another. The city is going quickly to hell, Rome has been falling a few thousand years, but people are nice to one another. Mithras too promises life after death, but only after a splendid ritual feast of life, no last supper with a boiled chicken and a few lousy matzos, and a friend who fingers you for the cops. In Rome the food is splendid.

The American President flew over me yesterday in a U.S. Army helicopter as I sat writing, on his way to visit the Papa. (The next distinguished visitor over there will be Kurt Waldheim.) It's the supply-side President who cut back on medical insurance so my eighty-seven-year-old mother has only twenty days to recover from a broken hip before she's sent to whichever government death factory has the first bed available. The theory is that stimulating the supply side of death will stimulate the demand for life. People will then avoid being sick, old, and helpless.

This is the country of mama and bimbo, despite the fact the Papa is celibate and the Mama is a virgin. That only makes baby more precious, a little god from heaven sent by carrier pigeon on lasers of light. You travel around Rome with a mother and baby and it's like travelling around with someone holding a panda. People spot it and literally start jumping up and down with pleasure, ladies, old men, teen age boys. In return when they grow up babies treat their mothers and other people like human beings. They like their mothers, they take care of them. My mother is heading for the death factory. Not much I can do about it.

San Clemente was the summer palace of Richard Nixon when he was king. I used to live nearby in Laguna Beach. Maybe that's why I'm reluctant to finally go to San Clemente, reluctant to confront there some undeniable but bluntly malevolent power.

It turns out that Signor Cranio really runs everything. Without arms or legs, he does it all with what he has—head, heart, and balls. There's a Capucin church in Rome with a catacomb of human bones used like tiles or any other material for mosaic, or rather assemblage, since the resulting decorations are often three dimensional, an arch of hip bones, rosettes of ribs, columns of femurs, a wall of skulls, vertebrae lamps. There must have been a premium on cadavers there for a while, a brisk trade in bodies. Cemeteries were exhumed, Capucin corpses commandeered for this grisly project reminding us of death to improve our lives. They had a supply-side problem, one which would have been no problem at all for modern methods. That's how Signor Cranio runs everything. Everyone knows he can supply as many cadavers as required with a wink of his eye. He knows how to stimulate the supply side. Is he a bad guy? Sure he's a bad guy. But at least he's up front, not sanctimonious. Sometimes bad guys are good. That's only human. As in Rome's cannibalistic jungle of stone, in his jungle every loss is a gain. Probably not mine or yours, in fact probably his. But what the hell, you can't have everything.

In the various archaic arenas around town they used to have bullfights, ancient swordsmen baiting maddened beasts to the shriek of crowds chanting "Cut the bull! Cut the bull!" Signor Cranio has cut the bull, sacrificing arms and legs to do so, which however he no longer needs. Now he just sits in his chair, all balls and brains, and talks his heart out. But the day his girlfriends turn on him his talk runs out. His talk does no good, nor do his screams.

That day begins when Nicolá in his black leather jacket angles up to Signor Cranio and whispers bad news in his ear. What follows I didn't see myself and only heard about through hearsay, so I can't guarantee its veracity. Nevertheless, what people say has its own kind of veracity, does it not?

They say that what Nicolá in his black leather jacket whispered to Signor Cranio is that one of their boys caught a fish that was too big to handle. Instead of throwing it back in the Tevere he pulled it out and now nobody knew what to do with it. They say that the boys cut off its head but it was still too big. It was a fish nobody had ever seen before, they didn't even know what it was called. After they cut off its head the exposed flesh, which was pink, began to bulge and soon took the shape of a woman's breast. The boys took it around to all the usual outlets but nobody would handle it. It was too big, but also there was something else. People were afraid of it.

Signor Cranio was not afraid of it. When they showed it to him they say he immediately tried to suck the breast part, but he couldn't seem to get his mouth around it, it was too big even for him. But that didn't mean he was afraid of it. He must have known, though, from that moment, what was going to happen to him, because he was the one responsible for handling whatever they brought in.

When my mother was helpless in the hospital she said to me one morning with obvious anguish, "I can't find Dad." My father had been dead for almost five years. (When my father was dying he went into a coma. He came out of it only once so far as I can tell. It was just after they took a tube out of his throat that was helping him breathe. At a certain point he suddenly sat up in bed and stared at my sister and me. He spoke in a voice that's hard to describe: loud, hollow, grating, almost a roar. Maybe it was because he'd had that tube down his throat, I don't know, but it sounded like a rush of wind through some distant cave of the netherworld. What he said in that roar, belligerently, as he stared at us with unseeing eyes was, "Go home, and go to bed!" He repeated it, with bellicose authority, emphasizing every word as if to leave no doubt about his meaning. "Go home, and go to bed!" Then he fell back and closed his eyes.) I can't find Dad. Then I discovered that workers in the hospital had stolen her diamond wedding ring off her finger, probably while she was asleep. That must have been what she meant. Later her false teeth disappeared.

They say that shortly after Nicolá came the boys came. As soon as he saw them coming Signor Cranio started singing. They say that as they knocked him off his wheel chair he was singing an old Italian folk tune with erotic off-color lyrics and endless variations that goes:

> Olimpia, Olimpia, Olimpia
>   Tu me tradisse,
> Me disse che te vegne
>   In vest' da Pise . . .
> Si Papa non vuole, Mama non dice,
>   Come faremmo fare l'amor?
> Si Papa non vuole, Mama non dice,
>   Come faremmo fare l'amo-o-o-o-r?

The tune of the chorus was later incorporated into Tschaikowski's "Capriccio Italien" just after the main theme, expressed by the trumpet solo, is punctuated by the full violin section.

Sometimes they ask me why I write this way when it would be so easy to give the audience a break and sell more books by using the kind of plot and character narrative they're used to. I write this way because it's a way of saying their whole system is bull. That's why I write this way. To cut the bull.

They say that as Signor Cranio lay on the ground they started kicking him in the head and the balls, and they say that as they kicked him he kept singing in his gravelly baritone. They say he kept singing even after someone had put a dagger through his chest. They say that he was still singing when his girlfriends came, vindictive as jackals, as he lay dying, and that to shut him up one of them put a knife in his mouth and cut his tongue out and they say in the neighborhood that even after that, as they pulled off his pants and cut off his balls, even after that, he persisted with a wordless song, or was it a scream, but song or scream they say he persisted in his aria until his last breath.

It was only then that the Carabinieri came to restore order. But they say that nobody who heard that song can forget it.

Name of the Dog

Name

Strange logics dictate the text of life. The first time I travelled to Europe, thirty-five years ago, the very first person I met on European soil was Federico Fellini. I was an admirer of his early films, among which *La Strada* had already made him famous in the States, but I did not yet know that his work was to become a major sanction for my own, because he had not yet produced *Eight and a Half*.

I had come over on the *Queen Elizabeth*. Five days in tourist class in the hothouse milieu of a giant ocean liner is something like being in summer camp. People you've never seen before become the target of feelings more intense than those aroused by close family members. There's something moving about such a voyage, possibly because the ship itself is always moving, churning up excesses of feeling completely inappropriate to the situation, which is, of necessity, terminally temporary. Add to that the fact that I was off on what was, for me, a great adventure.

Did you ever wonder what they did with the garbage generated by great ships like that? Not long before, I had been living near a huge garbage dump at the edge of Cambridge, Mass. I would watch the endless train of trucks coming in to dump their loads, exciting the gulls that swarmed the smouldering trash heaps like the flies of Beelzebub. At night greasy fires flared the steaming mounds of refuse with the redness of hell. And here we were in mid-Atlantic on a self-contained vessel with the population of a small city. By the end of the trip the *Queen Elizabeth* must have been a floating garbage dump.

Or did they throw it all overboard? Just the way the waste from the famous university town polluted its surroundings. I wonder about it now as I sit here at my computer in my comfortable apartment in

Paris where I live part of each year. Up on the rooftops I can see from my window that the crow that comes over from nearby Cemetery Père Lachaise is making uncustomary purring sounds, seductively musical, even poetic. Edgar Allen Crow.

The cemetery is where Jim Morrison is buried. His grave is the object of pilgrims from everywhere, but mostly from a sentimental mentality that makes of Dionysus an object of yearning, Dionysus, that now tired but mean, and still treacherous god. There's a story about Morrison hanging out at Max's Kansas City, the famous New York bar, when too lazy or drunk to go to the men's room, he pissed in a bottle under the table, and handed it to a starstruck waitress as a souvenir bottle of his leftover white wine. My informant always wondered whether she drank it.

The woman who arrived from the States this morning will stay over tonight at the Paris apartment. She reminds me of a girl on the *Queen Elizabeth*, I even remember her name because it was unusual. Nicki Nowse, rhymes with mouse, I had the impression it was an abbreviation of something Slavic. Both of them good-natured, lavish, voluptuous, neither was to become my lover. The version on the *Elizabeth* would finally offer herself to me, and in fact I was needy. When I turned her down she couldn't understand. Actually, neither could I. "I'm not used to men refusing me," she said. I wasn't used to women offering themselves. It was an offer I couldn't refuse. And yet I did. Why? Possibly there were other considerations in my life than the Dionysian, though if so, they weren't obvious.

But why beat around the bush? Naturally I can see today, from the vantage of all the time and experience since, and by a process of triangulation making use of the various evolved intelligences with whom I now maintain contact, that at that age I was suffering from a condition of repressed spirituality that relegated my moral, esthetic, and intellectual sensibilities to the unconscious. And the spiritual unconscious in a state of repression leads to a condition of spiritual perversion, in which the repressed impulses can only flare out in eruptive and often inappropriate ways.

At the time I met Federico Fellini I was still in love with a woman back in the States, though it would be more accurate to say that I was in sex, or in rut. The brute fact of sex, however, was only one factor in a relation that fulfilled repressed spiritual needs I probably didn't even know were being fulfilled, but whose satisfaction permitted release of the cruder but perhaps not more basic erotic impulses.

The very fact that I had left my lover for a year, knowing full well that the chances of picking up the relation when I returned were slim, in order to go off to Europe, shows that I must have been capable of being in love with something or things other than women at the time. Whether I knew it or not, and I didn't.

On the *Queen Elizabeth* I was in love with a blonde girl, not the buxom brunette who offered herself to me but a flat chested blonde girl with long straight hair who paid no attention to me. She looked very upper crust, the blonde girl, so I must have been in love with the ruling class, I must have been in love with power. Also, I was in love with the way the ship's prow pared back the ocean, with the pitch and roll of a vessel on the high sea, with the rhythms of the horizon through the round portholes, I was in love with the clouds climbing over the horizon, I was in love with the changing colors of the ocean, I was in love with the adventure of voyage. And I was in love with the idea of France, where I was headed, with the high tradition of European culture. But I couldn't admit any of this was love, maybe partly because, as I know now, it wasn't what we call love. The overload we put on that word just indicates the poverty of our vocabulary. No, it was something else. But I was unable to admit even its existence.

One very surprising development for me on board the *Queen Elizabeth* was my fascination with the person I referred to as The Wife of Bath. A vigorous English lady of a certain age, as they say in France—i.e., about fifty—she was invariably on the third-class sun deck of the ship holding what might best be called court. That is, sitting up in her deck chair, gripping a mug of tea, she told stories non-stop, stories peppered with peppery commentary, often of a bawdy nature, holding in thrall a shifting audience composed however mostly, I noticed, of her countrymen. I concluded that she must be a traditional type for them, something like our cracker barrel philosopher.

The most surprising thing for me about The Wife of Bath was her sexual frankness, a quality that probably offended many Americans at the time, but which the English on board seemed to take for granted. Outspoken commentary on sexual matters, witty, vulgar, unselfconscious, was the mainstay of her discourse. Hanging out the sex laundry was not something Americans were used to in the fifties, nor do we get much of that kind of erotic ventilation now without a sense of titillation or even naughtiness. Many of her stories were explicitly pornographic, and though many of them had some point, others were obviously just for fun. But they weren't sneaky or sick-oid. Her gusto was hygienic.

So The Wife of Bath suddenly opened a vision of another mode of life for me, one in which sexuality was no longer the dirty little secret that, because suppressed, became a point of reference for almost everything else. In America then sex was the repressed impulse behind power, behind morality, behind art, behind manners, behind mental illness, behind social structures, behind even and above all family life. How strange it all seemed after listening to The Wife of Bath for a while. What would Americans do without strug-gling with sex as evil? Would they be forced to struggle with evil as such? Have we spent so much energy on sex as evil so that we don't have to confront something else as evil? And if so, what?

In any case, next time you read Chaucer, look at "The Wife of Bath's Tale" from that point of view. It was with my lover back in Cambridge, where I'd been reading Chaucer for M.A. exams, that I first arrived at a state of total sexual satisfaction. Not that I hadn't been sexually active in my life, far from, but that was the first time I was aware of a sense of erotic fulfillment. This awareness came as if from outside of myself and not via my own reasoning powers, through the formulation that now I was ready to die. If necessary, that is. I can't explain this formulation. Why should I have been ready to die at the age of twenty-five, unless sex really has something to do with death?

It was in Cambridge that I saw Fellini's *I Vitelloni*, and there's an odd anecdote connected with that. I remember going to see it with my girlfriend feeling, as I said, contented as a well-used stud, we'd probably just gotten out of bed. But let me say something first about the life of a graduate student. Suspended as it is between the student world of the undergraduates and the professional life of professors, between the academy and the workaday quotidian, and above all, between the perfection of the written word and the abjection of the rotten world, it lacks what you might call ballast. Without friction with the ordinary contingencies and tolerating a high level of anxi-ety aggravated by too much work and too little pay, it tends to exaggerated swings of mood. So it's not surprising that going to see *I Vitelloni* in high spirits, I left the theater in a state of depression. Because in this story about young men trying, and failing, to break out of the banal provincial fate in which they're caught, I discovered the image of myself, and erotic accomplishments notwithstanding— which after all were in the province of any normal citizen—the prospect of my ordinary, mediocre, and meaningless life.

I thought Europe was the solution. In that, I was not very different from generations of American tourists. I was especially not very different from that great wave of American tourists starting with Henry James, through Gertrude and Ezra and "Tom" Eliot, and ending with Henry Miller, the so-called exiles, though nobody was chasing them out, who collaged together a museum curator Europe that never existed, except in the minds and, more important, works of those magnificent provincials, provincials more practical and clever than their supposedly worldly hosts. If Europe doesn't work right, why not fix it? No problem. Just rearrange history a little bit, jiggle some geography, and everything comes out the way you want. Now, of course, living here, I know that their idea of Europe was the illusion of colonials who, without realizing, had outgrown their colonizers.

Except for one thing. One reality they had firmly grasped and that I too had intuited in my own uncertain way amid all the cultivated nonsense pumped into my brain by museums and foreign films and institutions of higher learning. One bit of data, slight but crucial, instantly communicated to me when I met Federico Fellini on the train to Paris.

Coming out of the theater where I saw *I Vitelloni* with my girlfriend I was, as mentioned, feeling low. It was the movie, but it was the movie probably connected with some of the other facts of my life, my seedy apartment next to the garbage dump for one, my wage slave teaching job for another, which however little time it left me for my graduate work, was better than my imminent summer job which involved eight hours of lifting heavy railroad car parts and inventorying them, starting at seven A.M. I didn't know which was worse, the boredom of the inventorying or the exhaustion of the lifting but either way, when I got back to my rubbish redolent apartment I was in no mood to hit the books for the doctorate I didn't know if I really wanted anyway. But I would nevertheless get back into it, gradually, with long minutes spent staring at the burning garbage across the street until finally, with its stink in my nose, I was able to escape into *The Faery Queen* or some such, reading long into the night with never enough sleep for the railroad yard in the morning, I knew the routine, it was a routine that would soon put me into the hospital and knock me flat on my back for a good three months. Maybe I got sick because it was the only way consciously or subconsciously I could get out of it.

In some circumstances, maybe repression of the spiritual is a means of survival. I could have handled *The Faery Queen* without the railroad yard and the garbage. I probably even could have handled *The Faery Queen* and the railroad yard, or *The Faery Queen* and the garbage. But all three at once no doubt required a depth of repression that would have reduced *The Faery Queen* to another piece of work for processing by the academic mill, or maybe simply to garbage.

Anyway, coming out of the theater with my girlfriend, and here comes the odd anecdote now, there in the middle of genteel Harvard, which I was not attending, by the way, we passed a beat-up Chevy full of the kind of tough kids I was used to from Brooklyn, but which she, as a graduate of one of the Seven Sisters out of some upper crust boarding school, obviously didn't know how to deal with. And they whistled at her. Maybe they even hooted, or made some obscene remarks, I don't remember. As I quickened my steps to get out of there, she simultaneously stopped dead on the sidewalk, turned to me, and said in a loud voice, "Hit them!" Hit them. Five or six big guys from the slums. Probably with a few clubs, baseball bats, or other blunt instruments, and maybe some sharp ones as well. Oh yeah. Hit them.

But the odd thing about it, I felt at that moment as much in sympathy with them as with her. I could explain this, but do I really need to? In any case, the incident shed light. It was like being in, say, the Cinquecento in the Metropolitan Museum when all of a sudden a gigantic, muscular Mickey Mouse walks in, looking bellicose and confused. In the U.S. today, one percent of the population owns thirty-nine percent of the wealth, and the wealth of that one percent exceeds the total wealth of the lower ninety percent of the population. The numbers probably weren't so gross at the time, but the situation is endemic. It's not a situation that's unknown, but it's not sexy. It exists as data somewhere in the national psyche, maybe out there on the garbage heap of history, everything reacts to it but it's itself inert, down the chute, it's there but not there, out of sight out of mind, we don't want to think about it, it's garbage, rotting away, dead matter, one day it will kill us too.

No doubt all of the above was a subliminal factor in my willingness to leave my girlfriend behind for Europe, in search of a better world—what a laugh—though the decision had a perverse air of desertion to it. Even for myself. In other words, I felt guilty.

At the time, I was incapable of articulating any of this, even to myself. The only thing I had enough energy to think about besides getting my work done was getting back into bed with my girlfriend. Maybe that's what sex has to do with death. Until you have enough of it—and you never have enough of it—like death, sex keeps you from thinking about anything. Especially about death. Death, the last thing you want to think about.

Not that sexuality is necessarily negative. Far from. But it can be regarded as a negative and basically is by our culture, despite the way it's merchandised. Negative maybe because sex is not something that you normally buy, and in the marketplace anything that's free is suspect. And maybe it's exactly because it's regarded as negative that it imposes on us from all sides as merchandise. I mean, what's your reaction to a no-no? Yes, yes. Right?

But Fellini. The *Elizabeth* docked at Le Havre, and then you caught the train to Paris. Which I collected my baggage and caught. I settled myself in a compartment, and then decided I was hungry, so I made my way up to the dining car, which in those days was still a linen and silver scene. It wasn't as crowded as I feared it would be, probably most people knew it was overpriced, and I was immediately seated at a table whose four places already had two occupants. I nodded at the two people opposite and stared out the window, fascinated by the differences between the intensively civilized woods and fields of France and the random wilds and acreage of the States.

My tablemates continued their conversation, they were speaking French. And they were eating a big meal, I mean it was lunch time, but this looked more like a dinner that they had ordered, or less a dinner than a repast, an empty bottle of wine on the table, a bottle of mineral water, the whole bit, as I waited for my sandwich. They were up to cheese, and they ordered another bottle of wine to go with it. He was heavy featured, dishevelled but looked like he was congenitally dishevelled. Though he wasn't fat, as he appears to be in photos I've seen of him since.

Meeting Fellini is an incident stored in my memory much like a photo, or rather the negative of a photo taken long ago but not developed till recently, I haven't thought about it for years. In fact, you might say that the spiritual unconscious is a take on things stored like a negative that suddenly gets developed, or develops gradually, or may never develop at all. What agency snaps that original shot I leave it to you to contemplate. Maybe it's programmed into the genetic code, or simply part of the human situation. The negative, you might even say, is the mind's denial of the world's positive, its refusal to accept things as they are. The Fellini take has developed through the intervention of Edgar Allen Crow, who visits now and then from the cemetery, as a kind of memento mori. The thought of death, I probably don't have to tell you, tends to develop a lot of negatives that otherwise remain inert in the spiritual unconscious.

Gradually it dawned on me that they were talking about American film. I started tuning in, though my French was rudimentary at the time.

". . . Mickey Mouse," the woman said.

"And what was the name of the dog?" asked the man who I did not yet know was Fellini.

"Pluto."

"Pluto? The lord of the dead? What does that want to say?"

"It can to be that wants to say that it is as much serious as funny."

"If I remember myself well the name of the dog is Goofy. It is what?" Fellini asked.

"In Italian it is said ?potso," she said.

"Then, [?] it is to be dead to be crazy."

"How?" she asked.

"The dog."

The waiter came over to pour some wine. They stopped talking for a while to dig into the cheese. I was left to puzzle out this conversation. I found it a little mysterious. If the dog is dead to be crazy, who is the dog? And what does that mean? I could only guess he meant that death is a mad dog, which after all made some sense. In that, I mean, how do you deal with a mad dog?

I remember, even at this distance of time, that unaccountably as they were pausing for cheese and wine, my yearnings returned to the *Queen Elizabeth* and the girl with the long, straight blonde hair. At some point on board I had revealed my admiration for her to a shipboard acquaintance of her social ambiance, but who was trying to escape it. He expressed surprise when I singled her out. "You mean the white death over there?" he said. On the contrary, he expressed admiration for my buxom brunette. I never asked him what he meant by the white death.

Which leads me now to wonder what would have happened had I actually hooked up with the blonde and satisfied my needs for whatever I was unadmittedly craving by way of power and prestige. Because sex is never just sex, but always something else, the something else that in fact makes it sexy. Suppose I had been able to sate myself with whatever it was that I covertly desired, only to discover that wasn't what I wanted? That it was part of the garbage? My experience since suggests that would have been terminal. The white death. Mad dog country.

I was once attacked by a dog, a very large black and white dog something like a Great Dane, with jagged black splotches. It was somewhere in Spain. I was walking through some kind of wealthy neighborhood, the extremely substantial houses were mostly hidden behind whitewashed walls. I don't know why this huge dog was loose on the street, but it was, and it wasn't a stray either, it had one of those spiked collars. Out of nowhere, this dog started racing toward me with clear malign intent. Probably it felt its territory was threatened. Maybe for animals territory is the only identity. I couldn't think of anything to do other than keep walking slowly as if both unaggressive and unintimidated. The animal's head was level with the height of my shoulder. When it reached me it bared its slavering teeth and leaped in the air higher than my head, but instead of landing on me it dropped to the ground, never taking its eyes off me, and galloped on for another ten yards. Then it stopped, turned, and ran at me again, doing exactly the same thing. Strangely, it never barked, never so much as growled. It made four or five passes like that until I slowly walked out of the neighborhood. I can still recall the pattern of black splotches on its back and sides because they reminded me of a map of the British isles, the French coast and the Iberian peninsula. If I had a dog like that I would call it Europe. Or maybe my memory is playing tricks on me, maybe this is just the way, at some level, I feel about Europe. Even now I'm pitched into a state of combined defiance and anxiety when I give someone my name in Europe and they ask, "That doesn't sound American, what kind of name is that?" Reminding me that Europe still harbors much garbage that's never been sifted, much less recycled.

The network of evolved intelligences with whom I now maintain contact thinks that my meeting with Fellini had a hidden logic. In the sense that incidents materialize in the text of life only when your attention is attuned because your frame of reference makes space for them. This is what the network of evolved intelligences calls the grammar of incident, which it claims to know how to read. I might have sat next to Fellini all day and all night and never noticed him as Fellini. Or you might have. This goes for everything else, of course, from the moment you open your eyes in the morning and notice the light, which you wouldn't have noticed if you hadn't opened them. If you see what I mean. The evolved intelligences think that meeting Fellini was part of an ongoing reflex I had developed to avoid the white death. The intelligences think that for me white death avoidance had been reduced to a reflex for lack of conscious spiritual resources that probably would have made my life a lot more simple. Yes, I shoot back at the intelligences, but what do you expect from a kid still emerging from Lumpenville, U.S.A.? Mahatma Gandhi?

Edgar Allen Crow makes his presence known outside on the tiled roofs with a series of calamitous squawks that attunes my attention to a broader frame than the one my psyche reverts to if I'm not paying attention. Maybe that's his job, psyche tuning. I'm reminded of what happened next when I met Federico Fellini on the train to Paris. It was maybe then in my life that the something else not love, till then repressed, that often had moved me for unknown reasons to love things other than women, came first to my consciousness. What happened was I caught a phrase from across the table in the dining car that extracted me from my blonde reverie to focus, even eavesdrop, on their conversation.

"It is a species of ?contract with the spectators, is it not? As to *La Strada* or no import what spectacle. Yes, it is very ?owl. But [?] to my advice, in the sense where life is a piece of theater, theater is ?cowly [cow-like?] a piece of life, that also."

"It is necessary not to say that to [?]. Because if life is theater why you owe for entering?"

"Name of a dog! God pork! It is there, the problem."

"For what?"

"Let us admit because [?] not museum ?decay. It is only to think about life with respect and ?antagonism. [?] I not have envy to resist with ?understanding[?]. ?Garbage[?] [?] when I made *La Strada*."

What Fellini was admitting, insofar as I could understand what he was saying, was inadmissible to my American mentality at the time. He was admitting to the compulsive perfectionism of the spirit as against the abjection of the rotting world. He was confessing that the compulsion of the spirit was as inevitable as the garbage. The force of the to an American impractical if not intangible compulsion of the spirit is perfectly obvious when you think about it. *When* you think about it. The intelligences say that it is precisely because you don't think about it that you need to chase after the white death. Not, the intelligences will grant you, that Europeans don't chase after the white death, maybe they even chase it more, but at least they admit the helpless compulsion of the spirit as against the abjection of the rotting world.

This admission by Fellini, which I instantly if not consciously absorbed from what he said, and he didn't even say it, so I must have gathered it from the way he said what he said, was for me, according to the intelligences, one of those tiny turning points which you barely notice but which amplify and reverberate and shape the rest of your life.

I frankly don't remember what they discussed after that at the table in the dining car, but the minute I suspected that I was sitting opposite Federico Fellini, I knew I had to say something to him. Finally, as they were waiting for the change from the waiter, I blurted out in my abominable French, "Excuse me, sir, are you Federico Fellini?"

"Si?" he responded, a little defensively, I thought.

"I liked very much your film *La Strada*," I said in my abominable French.

Fellini nodded and replied in heavily accented English, "As long as the public likes it is the most important."

But I think he meant it.

Since those days, of course, Mickey Mouse has muscled into Europe in a big way. Out at Eurodisney near Paris it's still a question whether the public likes him. But Mickey is less confused now and knows what he's after. He's after Europe in the same way that Europe was once after the Americas. In the same way that the American exiles patched together their fairy tale of Europe, Mickey lays his fairy tale Europe of plastic castles over the real thing.

But what is the real thing? Maybe the real thing is no longer the actual flesh and stones of an ambiguous history but Mickey Mouse himself, now grown up and proliferating mickey mice everywhere. Maybe the real thing is what happens when the practical tom cats are away and the prodigal spirit starts to play.

About the Author

Ronald Sukenick has been on the leading edge of American writing for the past twenty-five years. His influence, however, is not confined to fiction. Through his writing about writing and his work as publisher and editor of the *American Book Review*, FC2/Black Ice Books, and *Black Ice* magazine, as well as his administration of the Nilon Award for Minority Fiction, he continues to foster and support innovative writers and to make their work available to readers.

Other Books by Ronald Sukenick:

Wallace Stevens: Musing the Obscure
Up, a novel
The Death of the Novel and Other Stories
Out, a novel
98.6, a novel
Long Talking Bad Conditions Blues
In Form: Digressions on the Act of Fiction
Endless Short Story
Blown Away
Down and In: Life in the Underground
Doggy Bag: Hyperfictions
Degenerative Prose (with Mark Amerika)
Mosaic Man
In the Slipstream (with Curtis White)